GREYFRIARS BOBBY
and the
ONE O'CLOCK GUN

George Robinson

Dedicated to Eleanor Atkinson
author of *Greyfriars Bobby*

CONTENTS

Chapter 1

BOBBY MEETS COLOUR SERGEANT SCOTT

Early in the morning as he left his lodgings to buy a pitcher of milk, Colour Sergeant Scott spotted a scruffy little dog sitting under a tree in front of Greyfriars Church. Expecting the dog to come running across, Donald shouted 'Here, boy!' but although the terrier was shivering with the cold, he ignored the command and remained firmly glued to the spot.

'He must be frozen stiff!' Donald thought. 'I'll fetch him a bowl of porridge.' Going back upstairs, he filled a bowl from an iron pot hanging over the kitchen grate and brought it down to the small grey dog who quickly lapped it up.

As he bent down to pick up the empty dish, Donald heard the sound of a wheelbarrow being pushed along the gravel path leading from the church to the main gate. Looking up, he spotted James Brown, the gardener, making his way to his bothy.

Shaking his head as he passed, the old man grunted. 'I widnae waste my time wi' that wee beggar if I were you! He came in through the gate connecting the kirkyard wi' Heriot's a few days ago, wi' a tin can tied tae his tail. The laddies at that school are worse than wild animals! Every time

I fling him oot, the shaggy wee devil sneaks back in again as soon as I turn my back!'

The following morning, as Donald got ready to go to work, he wondered if the terrier would still be hanging around the kirkyard. Putting on his scarlet tunic and buckling his belt, the colour sergeant picked up his pillbox cap. Polishing the leather peak with the sleeve of his tunic, he put it on, before heading downstairs to the front door.

Turning right, he made his way up the narrow cobbled lane leading to the church gate. Going into the kirkyard, he took a quick look round, but there was no sign of the little dog. 'I don't suppose we're likely to see him again!' he said to himself. 'The old man must have got rid of him at last. He probably chased the poor wee beggar back through the gate into Heriot's! The school gardener won't be too happy about that!'

Crossing Candlemaker Row, Donald headed along George IV Bridge to the Ordnance Survey office in Melbourne Place. The colour sergeant was a special kind of soldier. A surveyor in the Royal Engineers, he knew his job. He had been in the Army for over eighteen years and had mapped the streets of towns and villages all over Scotland and the north of England.

Horse-drawn carts and carriages moved slowly along the busy street as the morning traffic began building up. The pavements were filled with people hurrying to work or making their way to the shops. Following his usual routine, Donald bought a paper from the newsboy standing at the top of Victoria Street. Taking a quick look at the front page, he tucked the newspaper under his arm before crossing over to his office.

As he lived not far from the place where he worked, Donald usually returned to his flat during his dinner break. Leaving just before one, as he approached the junction at the top of Candlemaker Row and George IV Bridge, he found the terrier sitting on the pavement.

'What are you doing here, wee man? This is a surprise! You must have enjoyed that bowl of porridge I gave you! Now you'll be looking for your dinner! You'll need a name. I'll call you Bob!' Wagging his tail, the little dog barked and followed the colour sergeant across Candlemaker Row to his lodgings.

Although Donald's rank entitled him to quarters in the Castle's barracks, he preferred to stay in the town. Lodgings were hard to find in the centre of the city, and the rooms not occupied by the upholsterer and his family who lived at Candlemaker Row had been rented out to the colour sergeant, a retired businessman, a portrait painter and Mr Ritchie, an elderly tailor.

The tailor's door was open and as Donald passed his room, the old man who was stitching a pair of trousers on his sewing machine stopped work and took a look at the small dog. 'Who's this?' Mr Ritchie enquired. 'The regimental mascot, Donald? He'll have been sent up from headquarters to help you check the maps. He could do wi' a bath!'

'This is the dog I told you about. He's been hanging about the kirkyard. He's decided to accept my invitation and come in out of the cold.'

'He seems a canny wee beast. He looks half starved. He could do with something to eat! My daughter's made a pot of stew!' the tailor said, removing his glasses. 'Maria!' he called. 'Could you bring a bowl of stew through from the kitchen! Donald's brought a guest back wi' him!'

During the day when the colour sergeant was at work, and Bob was not patrolling the kirkyard looking for rats, the little dog would trot round the district, calling into shops where he was sure of getting a friendly welcome and a bite to eat.

Although Donald had named the terrier Bob, the locals preferred to call him Bobby. The butcher, baker and grocer were more than happy to provide the little dog with scraps of food, and whenever he fancied a saucer of milk, he would pay a visit to the local dairy.

Before deciding where he would dine, Bobby would trot through the main gate into the kirkyard and work up an appetite by chasing the cats who hung around Mylne's Tomb, in and out of the headstones. The terrier especially liked to call into a restaurant in Greyfriars Place, a few doors along from the entrance to the church, as he knew he could depend on a warm welcome and a hot meat pie.

When Bobby felt like it, he would even venture as far as the High Street. Attracted by the red painted engines, the little dog added the Fire Station at Fishmarket Close to his visiting list. The firemen were always glad to see him and the station cook never failed to provide Bobby with a tasty snack. Later in the day, when it started to get dark, the terrier would make his way back along George IV Bridge to the tailor's flat.

Keen on football, Donald never failed to watch the local teams in action when they played in the Meadows on Saturday afternoons. 'The regulars from the *Hole in the Wa'* are playing the gunners from Leith Fort, Bob! Fancy a trip to the Meadows after we've had a spot of dinner?' Getting up from the carpet where he had just settled down to take a nap, the terrier barked and wagged his tail.

Leaving the colour sergeant's lodgings, shortly after one, Donald and Bobby turned right at the foot of the narrow lane and headed along Forrest Road. Crossing Lauriston Place to the Meadows, they made their way down the path leading to the Boroughloch Brewery.

Although the weather was brisk, the sun was shining and the pitch was lined with spectators, well wrapped up against the cold. The gunners wearing pillbox hats, dark blue jerseys, white knickerbockers and red woollen stockings were already on the park, kicking the ball about as they waited for their opponents to turn up.

As Donald checked his watch, the *Hole in the Wa'* team trotted on to the field, wearing dark green jerseys, light grey knickerbockers and bright yellow socks. The team's captain who was wearing a brown derby, took off his hat and waved it confidently at the crowd as he led the players on to the pitch.

By the close of the first half, the artillerymen who spent their off duty hours playing football on Leith Links were leading five goals to two. As soon as play resumed, one of the gunners quickly took possession of the ball. Moving down the park at top speed, the bombardier's skillful display was terminated, when the opposing team's captain, tripped him up and brought him tumbling to the ground.

Staggering to his feet, the gunner took a swing at his opponent, blacking his eye and knocking off his bowler hat. Shouting and bawling, the angry fans flooded on to the pitch, eager to take part in the battle. 'Time we were heading back to Candlemaker Row, Bob! It's not just cats and dogs who like to scrap! If civvies want to fight, they should join the Army!'

As Donald and Bobby made their way along the path leading to Forrest Road, the colour sergeant spotted a pair of suspicious looking characters following an elderly man. Drawing closer, Donald suddenly realised that they were planning to rob his neighbour Mr Ritchie. 'Go for them, Bob!' the colour sergeant shouted, running to the old man's assistance, as one of the muggers knocked him off balance, while the other grabbed his watch chain.

Donald grabbed one of the villains by the shoulder, while Bobby sank his teeth into the other scallywag's leg. Although he struggled and twisted to get free, the thief was unable to escape from the soldier's iron grip. Managing to tear his leg away from Bobby's mouth, the mugger's mate took to his heels, leaving the terrier with a ragged piece of blue serge cloth clamped between his teeth.

A large crowd had gathered, curious to find out what was going on. A burly, red faced man with a black bushy beard held the villain's left arm while Donald gripped the right. Tossing a coin to a young boy standing at the front of the crowd, Donald instructed him to run up to the High Street and fetch the police. Clutching the sixpence tightly in his fist, the urchin ran off at top speed.

'Well done, Bob!' the soldier said, looking down at the terrier. 'You certainly gave these two toerags a run for their money!' Bobby wagged his tail and barked. 'Are you all right?' Donald asked, turning to the old man who was shaking like a leaf.

'The young devils!' Mr Ritchie gasped, trying to catch his breath. 'Thanks for your help, Donald. I dinnae ken what I would have done if you and Bobby hadnae come along. The thieving scoundrels were trying tae rob me!'

The street urchin returned accompanied by two policemen. One of the bobbies recognised the thief as he had picked him up before. 'Up tae your auld tricks, Harry! Now you're in real trouble! Ye'll no' just get a stretch in the Calton Jail. This time the magistrates will send ye' doon under and ye'll no' be coming back!'

As the bobbies led the mugger away, the tailor shook his watch and held it up to his ear. 'I think it's broken,' the old man said, his hand trembling as he showed the watch to Donald. 'I've had it for years. It's solid silver! My nephew Fred mends clocks and watches. He's got a shop in Leith Street. I'll ask him to repair it next time he comes to see me on one of his visits.'

'Let me hold on to it!' Donald suggested. 'We'll soon have it back in working order. Your nephew might be busy right now and it could be a while before you see him. I'll take the watch down to his shop on Monday during my dinner break and ask him to take a look at it.'

Donald looked down at the little dog. 'Ready to return to Candlemaker Row, Bob! We'd better see that Mr Ritchie gets home safely. It's been a busy day! You deserve a treat! We'll stop off at the butcher's in Bristo Street and buy you a juicy bone!' When he heard the word 'bone', the little dog licked his lips, barked loudly and wagged his tail to signal his approval.

Chapter 2

BOBBY AND THE TIME BALL

The following Monday, as Donald left his office just after twelve, he found Bobby sitting outside on the pavement. 'I'm taking the old man's watch to be repaired, Bob! Like to come along for a dander? I'll take you for a bite to eat when we get back.' The little grey terrier barked and wagged his tail, indicating that he was ready to go.

Heading down the North Bridge towards Waterloo Place, Donald and Bobby crossed over to Leith Street. Pointing to a large clock hanging from a bracket projecting out over the pavement, the colour sergeant looked down at his little pal. 'That's the shop, Bob! Number twenty five! Clockie Ritchies!'

Although the shop sold clocks and watches, a wide selection of jewellery and ornaments were also on display in the windows. Hearing the bell above the front door ringing, Frederick James Ritchie came through from his office. The proprietor knew Donald as he had met him on several occasions during his trips to Candlemaker Row to visit his relatives.

'Afternoon Donald! This is Bobby the Skye terrier who sleeps at my uncle's house, Sarah!' the clock maker informed his sales assistant, pointing to the little dog. 'I hope that Uncle Robert and Maria are keeping well?' he asked, turning to Donald. 'It's a few weeks since I paid them a visit. The shop's been so busy!'

Explaining that the tailor had been attacked in the Meadows, the colour sergeant assured him that he had not been hurt. 'He wondered if you'd repair his pocket watch,' Donald said, handing over the timepiece. 'It took a bit of a knock when the muggers tried to steal it.'

'I'll see what I can do!' Fred promised, opening the back of the watch. Taking a jeweller's eyepiece from his waistcoat pocket, he focused it on the mechanism. 'A nice watch! One of ours. Probably made by my father. It'll need a new balance staff and a good clean. Tell my uncle not to worry. I'll bring his watch over on my next visit.'

The sales assistant came through from the office. 'Don't forget you've got an appointment at the observatory,' she said, handing her employer his bowler hat.

'I hadn't forgotten, Sarah but thank you for reminding me!' the clock maker replied, taking a look at his reflection in one of the display cabinets after he had put on his hat. 'The Astronomer Royal depends on our craftsmen to maintain his clock,' he said, turning to Donald. 'We've never let him down. I'm going up to the observatory to check the master clock. It's running slow. Would you like to come along?'

'I'd like to take a look inside the building,' the colour sergeant replied as they made their way towards the door. 'It's an odd shape for an observatory! Reminds me of an old Greek temple! Fancy a trip to the Calton Hill, Bob?'

'I hope you're feeling fit, Donald!' Fred remarked as Bobby and the two men headed up Leith Street. 'We've got a fair old climb ahead of us!' Turning left into Waterloo Place, they crossed the bridge, heading for the steps at Regent Road which would take them up to the Calton Hill.

As they climbed the stairway, Donald looked up at the tall grey monument standing close to the summit. 'Looks like a giant telescope standing on end!' Donald observed as he tried to estimate the height of the tower. 'The building at the bottom looks like a miniature castle!'

'Aye!' Fred agreed. 'Admiral Nelson would have approved of the design. It was built to commemorate the Royal Navy's victory at Trafalgar. The White Ensign and the Admiral's signal are flown annually from the monument on the anniversary of the battle.'

'I'd guess that the tower is over one hundred feet high!' Donald estimated. 'The time ball must be visible from nearly every part of the city as well as the Firth of Forth!'

'That's about the height of it! That's why the mast was set up on the roof of the tower.' Fred explained, pointing to the huge black ball. 'The ships' captains have no difficulty spotting the signal through their telescopes.' Suddenly, without any warning, Bobby began racing up the path. 'He's in a hurry!' the clock maker said as the terrier took off at top speed. 'I see what he's after! He's spotted a cat!'

Surrounded by a high stone wall, the observatory sat on the summit of the hill, directly across from the monument. Pushing open the front door, the two men and Bobby made their way up the path towards the main building.

The astronomer's wife was standing between the pillars outside the front door. 'Thanks for coming along at such short notice, Fred. We've been expecting you! Could you take a look at the master clock? It's running slow.'

'May I introduce two friends of mine, Jessie?' the clock maker said as they made their way down the lobby to the observation room. 'This is Colour Sergeant Scott and his friend Bobby. I hope you don't mind me bringing them along. Donald was keen to take a look around. This is the first time he's visited the Calton Hill!'

'Of course not, Fred! The door is always open to the public and it's not the first time we've had a visit from a dog! Charles will be delighted to meet you both!' she added, bending down and tickling Bobby behind the ear. 'He loves animals. We'd keep a dog ourselves if we had time to look after it.'

'How are you Fred?' Professor Piazzi Smyth enquired, wiping his hands on a duster. 'I've just been cleaning the transit telescope! The smoke from the city's chimneys is definitely not an asset. Soot gets everywhere! If it gets any worse, I may have to consider transferring the telescope to the summit of Arthur's Seat!'

'I'm very well, Charles! Business could not be better. We're getting dozens of orders for clocks from railway companies, not only in Britain but all over the USA and India. I'm considering increasing my work force. This is Colour Sergeant Scott and his wee pal Bobby.'

'A pleasure to meet you, Colour Sergeant!' the professor said, shaking Donald's hand as he patted Bobby on the head. 'I see by your uniform that you're a member of the Corps of Royal Engineers. We're both in the same business. I chart the heavens and you map the British Isles!'

'I'll go out to the transit house and take a look at the clock.' Fred informed the professor. 'It shouldn't take a minute. I won't be long.'

'It's a good job that Fred's shop is located so close to the observatory,' the professor remarked as the clock maker made his way back up the lobby to the front door. 'It's absolutely crucial that the time ball drops at one. As you're probably aware, the correct time is absolutely essential when calculating longitude. If a navigator's chart was a fraction of a degree out, the vessel would end up miles off course. The master clock supplies the time automatically to the ball. My assistant Mr Wallace is just about to perform the daily drop. Would you like to accompany him over to the monument? He'll explain exactly how the lifting mechanism works. I'll let Fred know you're over in the tower when he gets back.'

'I certainly would!' Donald replied. 'I'd like to see the mechanism designed to raise the time ball up the mast. The ball must be fairly heavy to stand up to the gales blowing in from the Firth of Forth.'

As Mr Wallace and Donald made their way over to the Nelson Monument, Bobby took the opportunity to sniff around in the grass. The assistant drew Donald's attention to an insulated wire running up the side of the tower. 'Just before one, the master clock in the transit house automatically sends a signal along that wire to the locking pins holding the ball. The electric impulse releases the pins, allowing the ball to drop exactly on the hour.'

Climbing the stone steps leading to the front door of the building at the base of the tower, Bobby and the two men went inside. Mr Wallace nodded to an elderly woman who was down on her knees, cleaning the hall with a scrubbing brush. 'Mrs Kerr looks after the monument. She's lived here for years. She used to sell tea and coffee to the visitors,' the assistant explained as he guided Donald to the entrance of the stairway leading to the top of the tower.

'Mrs Kerr's certainly got her work cut out!' Donald remarked as he peered up the winding staircase. 'When she reaches the top, she must have to start all over again at the bottom!'

When they had nearly reached the room housing the lifting mechanism after the long climb up the narrow stairway, Mr Wallace pointed to a door. 'That's the entrance to the observation platform. The view is well worth seeing. It will also give you the opportunity to catch your breath. You've plenty of time before the time ball drops. Come upstairs when you're ready.'

Pushing the door open, Donald took a look outside. The sun was shining and the atmosphere was crystal clear. 'Take a look at this Bob!' the colour sergeant said, picking the little terrier up. 'It's like being up in an observation balloon!'

As Donald held him on the parapet, Bobby could see the Queen's Park, Arthur's Seat, Salisbury Crags and the Royal Mile stretching all the way from the Castle to Holyroodhouse.

Carrying the little dog round to the other side of the platform, Donald pointed to the paddle steamers and sailing ships heading up and down the Firth of Forth. 'In a few minutes from now, the ships' captains will be focusing their binoculars on the ball. They might have you bang in their sights right now!'

Going back into the tower, Bobby and Donald climbed the stairs leading to the small circular room containing the lifting mechanism. A square metal column bolted to the centre of the floor ran all the way up to the ceiling. Mr Wallace pointed to a metal plate. 'Maudslay, Sons & Field, London, 1853. That's the name of the company which set up the time ball a few years ago. They also designed the mechanism for the time ball at Greenwich.'

Bobby began barking as an electric bell suddenly started ringing. The assistant checked his pocket watch. 'Five to one!' he announced, going behind the column and turning the capstan wheel. 'Time to raise the ball!'

'The time ball is now positioned halfway between the base of the mast and the crosspiece,' Mr Wallace explained, removing his hands from the wheel. 'This sends the signal to mariners out on the Firth of Forth and the people of the town to prepare to set their chronometers, watches and clocks when the time ball drops.'

The sound of running water could be heard from inside the column. 'That's the rain water draining from the roof,' the assistant added. 'The water running down the pipe cushions the time ball when it slides down the mast at one.'

Three minutes later, Bobby barked as the bell rang and the assistant checked his pocket watch. 'Two minutes to one! Time to raise the ball again!' he announced, turning the capstan wheel. 'The time ball is now positioned under the crosspiece of the mast, ready for the drop!'

A fraction of a second before one, Bobby's ears pricked up as he heard the locking pins being released, followed by a swishing sound as the huge black ball slid down the mast. 'That's it! Bob's your uncle!' Mr Wallace declared. 'You can set your watch, Colour Sergeant! It's now officially one o'clock!'

Thanking the assistant for the demonstration, Donald looked down at the little dog. 'Come on Bob!' the colour sergeant barked. 'Down the steps. Quick march! Time to get our feet back on the ground!' After locking the door, the assistant followed Donald and Bobby down the narrow winding stairway, the sound of the colour sergeant's boots echoing off the whitewashed walls.

Fred Ritchie was waiting for them in the entrance hall. 'Would you like a cup of tea before you return to the office, Donald? I'm sure Bobby wouldn't say no to a biscuit. There's an excellent tea room at the top of Leith Street opposite Register House.' When he heard the word 'biscuit', Bobby barked and wagged his tail.

'What did you think of the time ball, Donald?' the clock maker enquired as the waiter arrived with their order.

'Fascinating, Fred,' Donald replied, as he stirred his tea. 'There's no doubt about it! A time ball should be set up in every town and port.'

'That's the plan!' the clock maker confirmed, selecting a biscuit from the plate and giving it to the little dog. 'With a bit of luck my company will get the contract to supply the electric clocks. There's already a number of time balls dotted around the world. In addition to Greenwich, time balls have been set up in Australia, India, South Africa and the United States. The system is absolutely essential for the safety of shipping. It won't be long before time balls are set up in seaports, towns and cities all over the world!'

As they left the tea room, the clock maker promised that he'd bring his uncle's watch next time he paid a visit to Candlemaker Row. 'I'd better get back to the shop!' Fred announced, glancing at the clock on the tower of Register House. 'When the cat's away the mice will play! Thanks again for bringing the watch. Glad you enjoyed your trip to the observatory. Come back again when you've time. The professor will show you how he uses the transit telescope to calculate the time for the master clock. Give my regards to Maria and my uncle!'

'Well, my wee man!' Donald said, looking down at the small dog. 'Tempus fugit! We'd better head back to Candlemaker Row. Time to get a bite to eat!' The little terrier barked and wagged his tail. Donald's words were music to his ears. He was feeling hungry. Although he'd enjoyed the biscuit Fred had given him, it was now well past one o'clock and he was looking forward to the meal he'd been promised for accompanying his pal to deliver the watch.

Chapter 3

THE 78TH HIGHLANDERS ARRIVE IN THE CAPITAL

Looking up from his newspaper, Colour Sergeant Scott took off his reading glasses. 'The Highlanders are due to arrive at the Castle tomorrow, Bob!' he informed his wee pal who was lying in front of the fire gnawing a bone. 'They've been abroad on active service for nearly twenty years. Fancy a trip down to the Waverley to see the troop train coming in?' Although it was February and extremely cold, the little dog barked and wagged his tail. He enjoyed going for a dander with his friend, as he knew that wherever they went, he was always sure of getting a bite to eat.

The following afternoon Donald finished work early. Returning to his lodgings, he knocked on Mr Ritchie's door to enquire if he had seen the little dog. 'Not since this morning,' the old man replied, looking at the clock on the mantelpiece. 'He must be down in the kirkyard. He can't be far away as he doesn't like being out in the dark.' Informing the tailor that he was going down to the station, Donald went downstairs to look for his wee pal.

Pushing open the church gate which had been left unlocked to allow visitors to take a look around, Donald went into the kirkyard. The walls of the kirkyard were overgrown with ivy. Stone dykes and rusty railings separated the graves from the main path. Many of the gates guarding the ancient tombs had fallen off their hinges and were now lying on the ground, bushes and tangled vegetation growing between the iron bars.

'I wouldn't fancy being buried here!' Donald observed as he made his way along the path. 'You'd need a razor sharp axe to cut those gates free. It's like being in the jungle! Dr Livingstone would have a job finding his way about!'

Placing his fingers in his mouth, Donald whistled to attract the little dog's attention. Pricking up his ears when he heard the signal, the terrier who was hunting for rats on the far side of the kirkyard, bounded down the path at top speed, barking and wagging his tail.

'I'm off to the station, Bob! Ready to go?' Pleased to see his pal, the terrier pawed the ground and barked to indicate that he was looking forward to the trip. As they made their way down the path to the front gate, half a dozen cats sitting in front of Mylne's Tomb scattered when they spotted Bobby trotting towards them.

Cutting across Candlemaker Row to George IV Bridge, Donald and the little dog joined the steady stream of men, women and children heading for the Waverley Station. Before crossing the High Street, Donald stopped at a barber's shop and peered through the window. 'Better nip in for a haircut, Bob!' he said looking down at his wee pal. 'Got to look smart. Headquarters staff including my commanding officer are sure to be at the station to meet the train.'

'Afternoon, Donald!' the barber said, pointing to the chair. 'Take a seat! The usual? Tidy up round the neck and side boards?' Trotting over to the corner of the shop, Bobby sat and watched as the barber trimmed the colour sergeant's dark brown hair.

'Like something on it?' the barber enquired, after he had brushed the cuttings from Donald's shoulders and held up the hand mirror to allow him to inspect the back of his neck.

'A touch of that stuff in the green bottle would be fine. Not too much. I don't want to arrive at the station smelling like Jenner's perfume department!'

The barber laughed. 'How about you Bobby? Fancy a trim, my wee man?'

'The weather's still a bit nippy,' Donald replied, removing his dark blue greatcoat from the coat stand and putting it on. 'I'll bring him in for a short back and sides before the summer arrives.'

As Donald put on his pillbox cap, the church bells began to toll. 'Better get a move on!' the barber advised, as the soldier and the little dog left the shop. 'That's the signal announcing that the train's due to arrive in half an hour!'

Crossing the road, Donald and Bobby headed down Market Street towards the Waverley Bridge. As he made his way down the steep hill, Donald looked over the railway line to the Scott Monument. Although it was now quite dark, he could see that the pavements on either side of Princes Street were packed with people.

Not only were the windows and balconies of the shops and houses along the city's main street filled with spectators, groups of men and women, muffled up against the cold were standing or sitting behind the parapets running along the tops of the buildings.

Turning left on to the Waverley Bridge, Donald spotted Fred Ritchie standing opposite the station entrance. 'Hello Donald! Nice to see you. I thought you'd be here!' the clock maker called as they made their way towards him. 'This is my wife Annie and our daughter Agnes. We couldn't bring Jamie as he's too young. We weren't sure if we should bring the bairn, but decided it would be a good idea as she's bound to remember an occasion like this when she grows up.'

'We'd better stand here, Bob. We'll never get down the carriageway now. Too many people!' Donald said looking down at the little dog. 'We should have set out earlier,' the colour sergeant explained to the Ritchies. 'Bob was out in the graveyard chasing rats!'

Agnes who was wearing a Tam o' Shanter, dark brown overcoat and tartan scarf, smiled and patted the terrier on the head with the Union Jack her father had bought from one of the street vendors, to wave when the kilties arrived. 'Nice doggie!' she said as Bobby backed away, deciding that he'd had enough.

'We'll get a dog when your brother's a bit older,' Mrs Ritchie promised. 'Fred fancies a Skye terrier just like the Queen's,' she explained as she wiped Agnes's nose with her hankie.

The city's Volunteer regiments had been brought in to line the route from the station to the fortress. Taking a look at the riflemen lined up at intervals around the curve of the pavement connecting the Waverley Bridge to Princes Street, Donald observed that the spacing between each man was far too wide. 'The Volunteers will have difficulty holding back the crowds, when the Highlanders march up the carriageway from the station,' he remarked to Fred. 'They should be positioned closer together!'

'You could be right, Donald. Have you also noticed that there are only a handful of policemen on duty?'

The Waverley Station was packed with people. The bandsmen of the County Militia and the Midlothian Coast Artillery stood at attention, ready to commence playing as soon as the train arrived, while the Lord Provost,

18

groups of high ranking military officers and civic officials waited patiently on the platform to welcome the heroes of Lucknow to the city.

As the station master checked his watch, the sound of the train's whistle could be heard in the distance. Two minutes later the locomotive pulling twenty eight carriages carrying the soldiers and their families steamed into the station.

Opening the carriage doors, the Highlanders wearing feather bonnets decorated with a white hackle, red doublets, McKenzie tartan kilts and plaids stepped out on to the platform. In addition to being equipped with an ammunition pouch, haversack, water bottle, bayonet and rifle, each soldier carried a black leather knapsack with a rolled greatcoat strapped on top.

The station porters lowered the doors of the railway vans carrying the officers' mounts, and the orderlies led the horses out on to the platform as the Highlanders lined up in formation. Receiving the order to commence playing, the crowds began to cheer as the bandsmen struck up "See the Conquering Hero Comes".

After the Lord Provost had welcomed the regiment's colonel, the officers mounted their horses. Receiving the order to move off, the Highlanders, drawn up in columns of four, shouldered their rifles and began the march up the carriageway towards the Waverley Bridge, led by the military bands.

As the escort marched towards the carriageway carrying the regimental colours, the station staff and the old soldiers standing in the crowd, removed their peaked caps and hats as a token of respect to the officers and other ranks who had died on active service.

Halfway up the carriageway, the drum major raised his mace, signalling the pipes and drums to begin playing. Excited by the sound of the pipes and the throbbing beat of the bass drum, the crowd's enthusiasm reached fever pitch when they spotted the regimental colours emblazoned with the battalion's battle honours being carried up the carriageway.

Waving hats, flags and handkerchiefs, the spectators pressed forward on to the roadway, pushing aside the soldiers stationed along the edge of the pavement to hold them back. Swamped by a mass of excited men and women, desperate to shake the kilties by the hand, the bandsmen were forced to stop playing. Unable to move forward, the column was brought to a sudden halt.

'I knew this would happen! Total pandemonium!' Donald shouted to Fred. 'Keep an eye on the bairn!' Mrs Ritchie frantically looked around, searching for Agnes who had been separated from her parents when the crowd surged forward on to the cobbles.

'Find her, Bob!' the colour sergeant barked. 'Go on boy! Find the wee lassie!'

Taking off like a bullet through the crowds, the terrier dodged and weaved his way through the forest of legs and feet. A few minutes later, although the signal sounded faint and faraway due to the noise of the crowd, Donald heard the terrier barking. 'Sound's like Bob's found the bairn!' the colour sergeant called out to the clock maker and his wife.

Making his way with difficulty through the tightly packed mob, Donald spotted the little girl standing in front of the park railings crying with fright. 'Good boy, Bob! You found the wee lassie!' Picking Agnes up, Donald carried the terrified toddler back to her parents.

Heaving a sigh of relief when she saw Donald returning with her daughter, Mrs Ritchie ran forward, bent down and hugged the little girl. 'Bobby found me, Mummy!' Agnes cried out. 'I've lost my flag!'

'Never mind, lassie! We'll buy you another one,' her father promised, putting his arm around his wife's shoulders to comfort her. 'I think we'd better take Agnes home, Annie. Thanks for finding her, Bobby! My wife and I are in your debt. Next time I come up to Candlemaker Row, I'll take you and Donald for a steak!'

Managing to push the crowds back, the regimental pioneers forced a passage through to Princes Street, allowing the Highlanders to continue their march along the city's main thoroughfare to the Castle.

'Time to return to Candlemaker Row, Bob!' Donald said, as the rear guard marched up the carriageway, followed by the horse-drawn baggage wagons. 'I don't think we'll see much more of the parade tonight. I think the lads are going to enjoy their stay in the city. It'll be a long time till they have to pay for a drink! Fancy a bite to eat before we return to Candlemaker Row?' Licking his lips in anticipation, the little dog barked and wagged his tail.

20

Chapter 4

BOBBY AND THE MONKEY

Although Donald could repair his own boots, he sometimes took them to a cobbler's in the Grassmarket as the owner came from Perth where the colour sergeant had been born. Deciding to pick them up during his dinner break and finding Bobby waiting outside, he took him along.

Situated in a valley between Heriot's and the Castle esplanade, the elongated square was the commercial centre of the Old Town. In addition to pubs, shops, warehouses and a brewery, the market had two banks where the farmers, horse dealers and carters carried out their business transactions.

The shops, stalls and merchant stores supplied everything from a needle to an anchor. Horse-drawn carts driven by the country carriers arrived regularly every day bringing eggs, poultry and farm produce from the outlying districts. Loading merchandise from the shops and warehouses, onto their wagons, the drivers carried the goods back to the people living in the small towns and villages outside the capital who depended on the service.

The market place was not only a commercial centre. Street singers, musicians, acrobats and jugglers entertained the public all year round. When the festive season arrived, the locals lined the pavements to watch the massive horse-drawn wagons belonging to Wombwell's Travelling Menagerie trundling into the square.

Jutting out from the Castle, the Half Moon Battery towered high above the market place. Garrison guns stood behind the battery's gun ports and a giant Union Jack flew from the fortress's massive flagpole.

When the gunners fired the garrison's guns to celebrate the Queen's birthday or to welcome an important visitor to the capital, the residents living in the tenements close to the battery could never be sure if the glass in their window frames would survive the ceremonial salutes.

Hearing the bell above his front door jangling, the cobbler came through from his workshop. 'Your boots are ready, Donald!' he said, taking them down from the shelf. 'You'll be wearing them to the banquet the city's giving for the Highlanders in the Corn Exchange?'

'Afraid not. Officers only!' Donald replied, looking through the shop window as the cobbler stuffed the black leather boots into a paper bag after showing him the heels. The windows of the tenements on both sides of the market place had been decorated with greenery and flags. 'I see the landlord of the White Hart's decorating the front of his premises.' Donald observed. 'It should be quite an occasion.'

'It certainly will! The Highlanders are being presented with their campaign medals. The politicians must be pleased. The sojers have added India to the Empire. I'm surprised that the Queen's no' been proclaimed Empress!'

'Aye! The businessmen and bankers might be happy, but there's a limit to the size of the British Army,' Donald replied, handing over the money for the repair. 'I'm not surprised that the lads are being treated to a free meal. They've been abroad for nearly twenty years. We'll come back later. The regiment has a first class pipe band. I like to hear the sound of the pipes.'

Putting the money into the till drawer, the cobbler took a look at the small dog. 'I've got some braw leather collars in stock. Here's one that would suit the wee beast up to the nines!' he said, showing Donald a brown leather strap fitted with a brass plate for the terrier's name.

Donald shook his head. 'He could do with a collar, but if I buy him one, it would look as if I owned him. Although I buy him his dinner, he's totally independent. Bob's got a lot of friends who provide him with meals. I'm not the only one on the wee beggar's list of benefactors.'

Making their way back up Candlemaker Row, as Donald and Bobby were about to turn the corner into the narrow lane at the top of the brae, the colour sergeant heard a voice calling to him from the opposite side of the street. It was Tam Cowan, the landlord of the *Hole in the Wa'*.

'My pub's being wrecked!' the publican cried out, as Donald and Bobby crossed the busy street towards him. The sound of breaking glass could be heard coming from inside the premises, while the regulars stood at the front door, terrified to enter. Followed by Bobby and the landlord, Donald took a look inside, expecting to find a gang of Irish navvies or a squad of soldiers from the Castle barracks creating havoc.

A monkey was scampering along the top of the mahogany gantry. Picking up a bottle of whisky, the angry little animal screamed and hurled it at the colour sergeant as he came through the door. Not content with throwing bottles, the monkey grabbed a stuffed pheasant by the throat, and tossed it on the floor which was covered with broken glass. 'Where in the name o' the wee man did you find him?' Donald asked, turning to the publican who was sheltering behind him.

'I bought him from one of the kilties up at the Castle!' the landlord moaned, removing his bowler hat and wiping his forehead with his handkerchief. 'Cost me half a crown! I should have my head examined! He's wrecking the place! Look what he's done tae my bust o' Rabbie Burns!' he moaned, pointing to the shattered pieces of the bard's head lying on the sawdust covered floor. 'It was my most treasured possession!'

'Have you got a sack?' Donald enquired, picking up a broom which the monkey had flung on the floor. Opening a cupboard door, Tam pulled out a canvas sack from one of the shelves and handed it to Donald who was pushing the monkey along the top of the gantry with the broom.

Annoyed at being poked and prodded, the monkey screamed with rage. Picking up a bottle of rum, he hurled it down at his tormentor. Gripping the broom tightly by the handle, Donald suddenly gave it a quick shove. Catching the monkey by the tail before he landed on the floor, Donald quickly popped him into the sack.

'If you're that desperate for a pet, I'd get a budgie or a parrot if I were you!' Donald advised Tam, handing him the sack. 'That wee beggar would be better off in the menagerie or the zoo!'

Later that day, Donald and Bobby went back down to the Grassmarket to see the Highlanders arriving at the Corn Exchange. The two-storey building which lay at the lower end of the market place between the brewery and the Vennel had not long been built.

The open windows of the tenements were packed with men, women and children waiting for the Highlanders to arrive, while the police patrolled the pavements which were beginning to fill with spectators. A juggler kept the crowds entertained by throwing a rubber ball high in the air and catching it in a cup strapped to the front of his head, while a street trader made his way along the crowd which was building up, selling Union Jacks.

A horse-drawn carriage drew up at the entrance to the Corn Exchange. Assisted by a footman, an elderly lady stepped down from the highly polished vehicle. 'That's General Havelock's mother,' an old man wearing a glengarry, standing next to Donald remarked. 'She'll be handin' oot the sojers' medals. Her laddie commanded the regiment during the Mutiny.'

Just after four o'clock, the sound of the pipes could be heard in the distance, signalling that the Highlanders were on their way from the Castle. Arriving at the market place, the soldiers wearing white shell jackets, kilts and glengarries lined up to be inspected before filing into the building.

'Well that's it, Bob!' Donald announced looking down at the small dog. 'I hope the lads enjoy their dinner. They've certainly earned it! They've been abroad a long time. Time we were heading back to Candlemaker Row!'

On the way back to his lodgings, Donald decided to stop off at the *Hole in the Wa'*. The public house was packed. Most of the regulars knew Bobby as they lived in the area and greeted the little terrier as he trotted in. 'I appreciate the help you gave me with the monkey, today, Donald! What would you like to drink?' the landlord enquired, wiping the top of the bar with a cloth. 'It's on the house!'

'I'll have a dram and Bob wouldn't say no to a saucer of milk,' Donald replied, winking at the little dog. Bobby barked, pawing the sawdust as he wagged his tail.

'Bella will also bring the wee dog a bite to eat,' the landlord said, instructing the barmaid to pour Donald a nip. 'In future when Bobby comes in, he'll be guaranteed his lunch. No charge! You can count on that!'

'There you go Bob! Did you hear that?' Donald said to the little dog who was shaking the sawdust off his coat after rolling about on the floor. 'Thanks to the monkey you can add the *Hole in the Wa'* to your list of restaurants, pubs and shops. Who said that there's no such thing as a free dinner!'

While Bobby got stuck into the bowl of tasty scraps the barmaid had prepared for him, Donald asked the landlord what had happened to the monkey. 'I took your advice and decided to let the little devil go,' the publican replied. 'He's got a new owner. They're through the back playing dominoes. Have another dram!'

Carrying his glass through to the smoke filled room at the rear of the pub, Donald spotted the monkey sitting with Coconut Tam and his pals, including the juggler who had been performing in the Grassmarket that afternoon.

Donald looked at the monkey. He was pleased to see that this wasn't the angry little animal who had tried to demolish the premises earlier that

24

day. The cheeky little chap looked quite content as he nibbled on a piece of coconut and watched his new friends playing dominoes.

Emptying his glass, Donald turned and looked down at the terrier who had trotted through from the bar to join him. 'Finished your supper, Bob? Maria and her father will be wondering where you've got to. We'd better get across the road before they call out the police. Say good night to the monkey!'

'Which one dae ye mean, Colour Sergeant?' Coconut Tam enquired, chapping on the table as he spat on the floor. 'The *Hole in the Wa*'s full o' them! Especially the fitba' team!'

Chapter 5

BOBBY AND THE TIME GUN

Colour Sergeant Scott put down his pen and looked up at the clock. It was nearly one and time for his dinner break. As he closed the door leading to the hallway, he was approached by a small dapper man wearing a top hat and dark grey overcoat.

'Colour Sergeant Scott, I presume?' the businessman said, holding out his hand. 'Allow me to introduce myself. My name is John Hewat. I'm a member of the Edinburgh Chamber of Commerce. I've just come from a meeting in our rooms upstairs. We're planning to set up a time gun which will fire a signal at one o'clock.'

'A time gun?' Donald replied. 'The city has a time signal. The time ball on the Nelson Monument provides an accurate signal to shipping in the Firth of Forth!'

'The Chamber was responsible for setting up the time ball several years ago,' the businessman explained. 'Although the system is extremely efficient, the ball can be difficult to spot in foggy weather. I submitted the proposal after observing a time gun firing some years ago in the Palais Royal Gardens during a business trip to Paris. The Astronomer Royal for Scotland is also in favour of an audible signal. Colonel Maclean at Leith Fort has offered to supply a garrison gun, while Fred Ritchie, the proprietor of James Ritchie & Son, is in the process of building a clock to fire it.'

'That would explain the sound of gunfire coming from the Castle last week,' Donald replied, as they made their way along the hallway to the front door. 'The Royal Artillery must be carrying out tests.'

'That's correct! The Chamber plans to print a map showing the time in various parts of the city when the gun fires. Not only will the map be published in the street directory, copies will be issued to the residents, shopkeepers and businessmen. Can you advise me which department to contact for permission to use an Ordnance Survey map?'

'Certainly, sir! You'll have to apply to the head office at Southampton,' Donald assured him, opening the front door and following him out. 'I'll instruct my clerk to supply your secretary with the details when I return from my dinner break.'

'Looks as if you have another customer requiring your assistance!' Mr Hewat observed as they left the building, pointing to the little dog who was sitting outside.

'That's Bob. He first appeared in Heriot's school grounds a couple of years ago. No one knows who he belongs to,' the soldier explained. 'He's got into the habit of following me back to my lodgings during my dinner break.' Thanking Donald for his assistance, the businessman climbed into the horse-drawn cab waiting for him at the kerb.

As they crossed Candlemaker Row, Donald spotted Fred Ritchie who was making his way down the narrow lane leading to the main gate of the church. 'Afternoon, Donald! How are you? I've just been visiting my uncle,' the clock maker said, bending down to pat the terrier on the head. 'Bobby's looking bright eyed and bushy tailed. He must be getting plenty to eat!'

'He should be! He gets fed everywhere he goes! The wee beggar's got an appetite like a Clydesdale horse. Have you any idea when the Chamber of Commerce plan to set up the time gun? I've just been asked if the Ordnance Survey office can supply the Chamber with a map.'

'As soon as possible. The project is well advanced. The master gunner has been carrying out tests to find a suitable spot to site the gun. He'll also have to determine the correct size of charge to use. As you know, too big a charge could result in the windows of the shops and tenements in the vicinity of the Castle being shattered!'

'Why use one of the Castle's guns?' Donald asked. 'One of the Russian guns standing next to the Nelson Monument could be used to fire the signal!'

'That would be more convenient, I agree, but firing a gun from the Calton Hill would upset the observatory's instruments. The Astronomer Royal has enough on his plate keeping the observatory running, without the Royal Artillery adding to his trials and tribulations! We'll have to use one of the Castle's guns. We have no choice! That's why the gunners are carrying out tests. When you get the chance, come down to the shop and I'll show you the electric clock we've designed to fire the gun.'

The following day, keen to see the clock, Donald decided to go down to Leith Street during his dinner break. Finding Bobby sitting on the pavement outside his office, he took him along.

The clock maker was attending to a customer as the colour sergeant and Bobby came into the shop. 'Afternoon, Donald. You'll have come to see the clock. Go on down to the workshop. I'll be with you in a couple of ticks! It's the sales assistant's day off!'

Going downstairs, Donald took a look inside the workshop. Busy concentrating on repairing watches and clocks handed in by customers, the craftsmen looked up briefly before getting on with their work. An apprentice with red hair and freckles sat on a stool in the corner polishing a brass dial which had just been removed from a grandfather clock.

Bobby cocked his head and barked in surprise as a small bird popped out of a clock designed like a chalet and signalled the time before disappearing behind the tiny wooden doors. 'That's a cuckoo clock, wee man!' the apprentice explained, laying down his shammy. 'Made by the clock makers in the Black Forest. If you're wondering where the wee gowk's gone, you'll have to wait for another fifteen minutes until he pops out again!'

'This is it, Donald!' Fred announced with pride pointing to a clock standing in the corner, when he came into the workshop ten minutes later. 'The clock designed to automatically fire the One o'clock Gun! This clock will make the name of James Ritchie & Son famous all over the world! Like the cabinet? A nice piece of wood. No doubt the gunners will paint it regulation grey as soon as it's placed in position!'

Removing the weight hanging from a metal lever, Fred handed it to Donald. 'When the weight falls at one, it pulls the lanyard attached to the friction-tube, igniting the charge and firing the time gun. As the time gun and the ball will be connected to the same circuit, the time ball will drop as the gun fires. Even if the weather's cloudy and the ball can't be seen, the sound of the gun will still be heard over a wide area. In addition to the clock, we've also offered to supply the batteries free of charge.'

'How will the time signal be sent from the observatory to the clock at the Castle? The wire will have to be attached to the buildings,' Donald said, taking a closer look at the mechanism inside the cabinet. 'That'll be a costly business. You'll need permission from the property owners. It could take years!'

'That's correct!' Fred agreed. 'To overcome the difficulty, we've decided to connect an overhead cable between the Nelson Monument and the Castle in a single span. Our calculations show that the wire will have to be over four thousand feet long.'

Donald looked at the clock maker. He could see that Fred wasn't joking. 'We'll hire a crew of sailors from Leith to rig the cable. We hope to get under way early in April. I'll let you know when the project starts.'

As promised, Fred Ritchie sent one of his apprentices up to Candlemaker Row the following month with a note informing Donald when the work would begin.

Rising at the crack of dawn on a sunny April morning, while the residents and Bobby were fast asleep, Donald left his lodgings. Crossing Candlemaker Row, he headed along George IV Bridge. Turning left at the corner of Melbourne Place, Donald made his way up the Lawnmarket towards the esplanade.

There was not a cloud in the sky and as he headed up the parade ground towards the wooden stockade, Donald could see a group of golfers teeing off on Bruntsfield Links. 'They must be keen,' Donald said to himself, as he looked up at the flagpole on the Half Moon Battery. 'The Union Jack's not even flying!'

Nodding to the kilted sentry, Donald crossed the drawbridge leading to the main gate. Climbing the cobbled brae towards St David's Tower, the soldier made his way through the Inner Gate to the Argyle Battery. As he approached the battery, the colour sergeant spotted Fred Ritchie standing below the watchtower, deep in conversation with Professor Piazzi Smyth, Master Gunner Findlay and a bearded gentleman holding a map.

'Morning, Donald! Glad you could make it. It's a lovely day. You're already acquainted with the professor and Master Gunner Findlay. This is Mr Newall,' the clock maker said, introducing the gentleman with the map. 'Mr Newall is the proprietor of the firm which manufactures the telegraph cable being laid across the Atlantic. He's been kind enough to come along and help supervise the rigging.'

'You're a sapper, I see!' the factory owner observed, shaking Donald by the hand. 'A pleasure to meet you, sir! My company supplies the Corps with telegraph wire. Only the finest steel has been used to produce the seven strands of wire used in the manufacture of the cable about to be connected from the fortress to the monument,' he explained, pointing at the drum.

'The Royal Engineers have given permission to set up a windlass and gearing inside the watchtower,' Fred added. 'The cable is attached to a rope. As the cable unwinds from the drum, the riggers will carry the rope through the streets to the Calton Hill. Ready to get under way, Ned?' the clock maker called to the weather beaten old salt in charge of the riggers, who was standing by the watchtower door.

'Aye, aye, Captain!' the sailor replied, raising his hand in salute as he began to turn the handle of the windlass. 'Dinnae worry! We'll get the job done. If a cable can be laid along the sea bed from Calais to Dover, we should be able to string a wire from the Castle tae' the Admiral's tower!'

'The riggers will carry the rope to the head of the Mound, through East Princes Street Gardens to the Waverley Bridge.' Fred explained. 'From the Waverley, the rope will be hoisted on to a tenement roof at the foot of the North Bridge, across to the post office building at Waterloo Place and then to the Nelson Monument, where it will be attached to a windlass set up on one of the windows. The riggers will then tighten the rope, raising the cable off the ground, high above the city. The rigging crew's got a difficult job ahead of them.'

'The matelots have certainly taken on a mammoth task!' Donald replied, taking out his watch to check the time as reveille sounded and a lance corporal raised the Union Jack on the Half Moon Battery. 'Connecting the Castle with the Nelson Monument's going to require a lot of skill if the riggers are to avoid uprooting the trees in Princes Street Gardens! Time I was getting back to my lodgings! It's six o'clock!'

Thanking Fred for inviting him along, Donald set off at a brisk pace for Candlemaker Row as he knew that Bobby would be wide awake and waiting for his breakfast.

Chapter 6

THE FIRING OF THE ONE O'CLOCK GUN

The following month, as Donald sat at the kitchen table polishing his boots, Bobby barked loudly. Seconds later the colour sergeant heard a knock at the front door. 'That'll be the postie, Bob!' Donald said, looking at the clock on the mantelpiece. Laying his boots down carefully on the carpet, he got up from his chair and went downstairs to pick up the mail.

'It's probably a bill, Bob!' he said as he opened the flap. The envelope contained an invitation from the chairman of the Edinburgh Chamber of Commerce inviting Colour Sergeant Scott to attend the official firing of the One o'clock Gun. A note enclosed with the invitation, thanked Donald for his help in providing the address of the official who had given the Chamber permission to use an Ordnance Survey map.

A few weeks later, as Donald left his office to attend the ceremony which was to be held in the observatory's grounds, he found Bobby waiting for him outside on the pavement. 'Afraid you can't come, Bob,' he informed the little dog. 'The invitation only admits one!'

Crossing over to the High Street, as Donald made his way past St Giles, he suddenly got the feeling that he was being followed. Turning round he found the terrier trotting along the pavement a few feet behind him. 'He must think I'm heading for the clock makers in Leith Street!' Donald thought. Although he pointed his swagger stick at the little dog, and ordered him to return to Candlemaker Row, Bobby ignored the command and continued to follow him down the Royal Mile.

'You win! Don't blame me if the chairman sends for the dog catcher when he sees you trotting into the observatory grounds!'

As they made their way down the North Bridge, Donald pointed to the cable connecting the clock at the Castle with the Nelson Monument 'That's the halfway point, Bob! It's an amazing achievement. I hope the wire doesn't snap with the strain. If it does, Fred's company will have some job fixing it.'

Although the passengers sitting on the top deck of a horse-drawn omnibus craned their necks to see what Donald was pointing at, it was difficult to spot as the cable which hung in a huge arc over the city was only an eighth of an inch thick.

When he arrived at the observatory, Donald found the grounds inside the enclosure packed with guests. Although the Lord Provost, the Provost of Leith, scientists and civic officials were formally dressed in top hats and frock coats, while the military officers wore full dress uniforms, many of the male guests had decided to wear lightweight summer suits. The female guests dressed in crinolines and bonnets carried parasols to protect themselves from the sun.

The guests passed the time admiring the magnificent view over the Firth of Forth as they waited for the time ball to be raised. There was not a cloud in the sky. The white-walled cottages of the fishing villages dotted along the coast on the far side of the firth could clearly be seen, while the midday sun reflected from the sails of the steady stream of vessels heading up and down the busy estuary.

As Donald and Bobby made their way through the crowd, the soldier spotted John Hewat. 'Glad to see you, Colour Sergeant Scott!' the businessman said shaking his hand. 'I see you've brought your little friend along to witness the historic event!'

'I tried to stop him but he's a determined wee devil. He's got a mind of his own!'

'I can see that! I'm glad he decided to grace us with his presence. Terriers are reputed to bring good luck. Our guests will be having a glass of wine after the time gun fires!' The businessman looked down at the little dog. 'We'll also get you a bite to eat. I have it on good authority that you're extremely fond of your food!' Bobby barked and pawed at the grass with his back leg.

Handing Donald one of the time gun maps, John Hewat pointed to a series of circles which had been printed around the Castle. 'The lines indicate exactly when the sound of the time gun reaches those specific areas. Master Gunner Findlay has decided to use the twenty four pounder standing next to the flagpole on the Half Moon Battery to fire the signal. The professor has moved the master clock which stood in the transit house inside the observatory.'

Over on the Half Moon Battery, watched by Fred Ritchie and supervised by Master Gunner Findlay, the gun team consisting of a bombardier and gunner wearing dark blue shell jackets and pillbox caps prepared to load the time gun. 'Ready lads!' the officer said, checking his watch with the time gun's clock, 'It's ten to one!'

Placing their hand spikes under the hubs of the wheels, the gunners rolled the time gun back from the gun port. Picking up a rammer, the gunner pushed a cloth bag filled with gunpowder down the barrel. Using their hand spikes, the gunners rolled the time gun back to its original position on the gun port's apron.

Inserting the friction-fuse into the gun's vent, the bombardier drew the cord attached to the weight inside the clock from the side of the wooden cabinet. Pulling the lanyard over to the time gun, the soldier hooked the cord to the metal ring on the friction-tube.

Over on the Calton Hill, Professor Piazzi Smyth stood at the top of the steps leading to the observatory. 'Ladies and gentlemen! Can I have your attention! The time ball is now being raised halfway up the mast!' the astronomer announced, pointing to the top of the tower. 'In exactly three minutes, the ball will be raised to the crosspiece! The countdown will begin at thirty seconds before one, allowing you to check the accuracy of the signal with your watches. This is a historic moment! Prepare for the sound of the gun firing when the time ball drops!' he added before going into the observatory to check the master clock.

The spectators held their breath, trying with difficulty to focus on the Half Moon Battery, the time ball and their watches as they waited for the loud bang which would be heard throughout the city and by the ships' crews out on the Firth of Forth.

As the time ball slid smoothly down the mast, Bobby began barking with excitement. Although the guests had prepared themselves for the sound of the report, followed by a puff of white smoke, the twenty four pounder standing on the Half Moon Battery remained silent. 'I knew this would happen!' one of the guests who must have had a crystal ball in his pocket, exclaimed.

Amused by the remark and the racket Bobby was making, the guests started laughing, relieving the tension which had built up during the countdown. Emerging from the observatory, the professor addressed the crowd. He explained that although the time gun had failed to fire, the possibility had been taken into consideration and asked the guests to return at the same time the following day to witness the second attempt.

Over on the Half Moon Battery, Fred Ritchie checked the time gun's clock, while the master gunner examined the vent. Removing the friction-tube from the time gun's vent, the artillery officer examined it closely. 'Looks as though the fuse might be faulty! You'd better get over to the observatory and inform the professor. I'd take the friction-tube with you,' the master gunner said, handing Fred the copper cylinder. 'The reporters will want to know the details. Don't worry! We'll try again tomorrow. Second time lucky, old chap!'

The following day as he was about to leave his office, Donald looked up at the clock. As the second hand approached one, he took out his watch, expecting to hear the signal. Going over to the window, he looked out into the street. Only the sound of the traffic could be heard as the horse-drawn carts and carriages clattered over the cobbles. 'Looks like the time gun's failed to fire again!' he said to the office clerk.

'Looks like it!' the clerk replied, opening his desk drawer and taking a cheese sandwich from his lunch box.

Opening his newspaper the following morning, Donald found the reason for the time gun's failure. According to the report, the friction-tube was not to blame, the door of the clock had accidently been left open, allowing dust to blow in, disabling the mechanism.

A third attempt to fire the signal was to take place that day. As Donald left his office, he found Bobby waiting on the pavement. 'Think the time gun will fire today, Bob?' he said, looking down at the little dog. A loud bang like the crack of thunder suddenly exploded from the Half Moon Battery, halting the pedestrians dead in their tracks. Flocks of startled pigeons shot up like rockets from the sandstone buildings where they had been perching.

Donald checked his pocket watch. 'Bang on time!' he confirmed. 'Success at last, Bob! It's officially one o'clock! Not only will the ships' captains and station masters be able to check their chronometers and watches, you now have a signal, telling you when it's time to go for your dinner!'

Barking excitedly, Bobby wagged his tail. The little dog was feeling hungry. It was one o'clock. He couldn't wait to get back to the restaurant at Greyfriars Place for a hot meat pie.

34

Chapter 7

THE DISASTER IN THE HIGH STREET

Colour Sergeant Scott knelt in front of the fireplace heating a tablespoon filled with lead. It was not long till Christmas, and he was casting lead soldiers for the toy shop in Greyfriars Place. Pouring the lead into the mould, Donald pulled off the glove he was wearing to protect his hand and waited for the molten metal to cool. Pulling the two halves of the mould apart by the wooden handles, he carefully removed the tiny figure. 'Another recruit!' he said, showing the Prussian grenadier to the little dog. 'Time to call it a day, Bob!' he added, looking at the clock.

Shortly after two, Donald was wakened by the sound of people shouting in the street. Pulling on his blue serge trousers he went through to the parlour to find Bobby sitting in front of the fire, wide awake. 'I wonder what's going on, Bob? Sounds as though a fire's broken out!'

Returning to his room, he pulled on his boots and put on his greatcoat and pillbox cap before going downstairs to the front door. Spotting the landlord of the *Hole in the Wa'* standing outside the pub, Donald and Bobby crossed over to Lindsay Place. 'A tenement in the High Street's collapsed!' the publican said. 'Didn't you hear the tremendous crash? It must have been heard as far away as Portobello! The noise was ten times louder than the One o'clock Gun!'

Wearing overcoats over their nightgowns, Maria and her father came downstairs from their flat and crossed the street to find out what was going on.

'The landlord reckons that a tenement's collapsed in the High Street! I'd better go along and see if I can help!'

'It sounds serious! They'll need all the help they can get. I'd better take father back upstairs before he catches his death of cold. Be careful, Donald! We'll have a cup of tea ready for you when you return!'

Joining the steady stream of people hurrying along George IV Bridge, Donald and Bobby turned right at the top of Melbourne Place and headed down the High Street. When the colour sergeant arrived at the scene of the disaster, he could hardly believe his eyes.

The front wall of the tenement had totally collapsed. Although the floors had disappeared, the tenants' clothes covered with dust still hung from pegs on their hangers, and fires lit the previous day smouldered in the grates on the gable walls, which were still standing. Buried under tons of rubble, the shops at the foot of the tenement were no longer visible.

Barricades had been set up across the street to keep back the crowds, and the glass bowls on the municipal gas lamps removed, to provide as much light as possible to enable the firemen and volunteers to search for survivors. Squads of soldiers had been sent down from the barracks at the Castle to assist the police control the crowds, while volunteers carrying flaming torches helped the firemen to sift through the wreckage.

'Morning Donald!' Fire Master Mitchell said, removing his helmet and wiping his forehead with his handkerchief as he approached the barricade. 'As you can see, we've got a real disaster on our hands! The building collapsed like a pack of cards shortly after one! The tenement should have been condemned years ago. It must have been over three hundred years old. Can we borrow your dog?' he said looking down at Bobby. 'There's no animal on earth like a terrier when it comes to rescue work!'

'Go on Bob!' Donald instructed the little dog. 'See what you can find!' Shooting off like a bullet under the barrier, Bobby made his way over the debris, eager to join the firemen and rescue workers searching through the mounds of rubble. Tunnelling under the piles of wooden beams and joists, the little dog worked his way through the wreckage. Suddenly he started barking.

'Looks like he's found something!' one of the firemen shouted, scrambling over the rubble towards the little dog. Climbing over the shattered timbers, stonework, plaster and broken furniture, the firemen headed towards the terrier who was frantically digging under a massive wooden beam.

Spotting a human foot covered with a red sock sticking out of the rubble, one of the firemen bent down to take a closer look. Turning to his mates he urgently signalled them to come across. 'There's somebody trapped down here! I can hear a voice calling for help!' Cupping his hands to his mouth he bawled back. 'This is Fireman McMurtrie! Edinburgh City Fire Brigade! Who are you?'

'I'm fine! How are you?' piped a voice from under the rubble. 'My name's John! John Geddes!'

'At least he's still got his sense of humour!' the fireman remarked. 'Hold on, John! We'll soon have you out! First we've got to move a heavy beam! Are you okay?'

'Heave away, lads!' John bawled back. 'I'm no' deid yet!'

Using a two-handed saw, the firemen began cutting through the heavy wooden support. When the massive obstacle had been removed, armed with picks and shovels, the rescuers started digging. Carefully easing the youngster out, Fireman McMurtrie asked John, whose face was covered with blood, how he was feeling.

'Fine! It's cauld the night!' John replied, pulling the remains of his tattered nightgown down from around his neck. 'Nothing seems to be broken, but my mouth feels like Portobello beach. I could dae wi' a drink o' water! Thanks for pulling me out! Have you seen my other sock?'

'You can thank the wee dug for saving your life!' the fireman said, as he helped lift the youngster on to a stretcher. 'He spotted your foot sticking out of the wreckage!'

'Well done!' remarked a gentleman who had been watching the terrier searching through the debris, when Bobby trotted back under the barrier, his coat covered with dust and pieces of plaster. 'That's an intelligent animal you've got there, Colour Sergeant! He looks like a Skye terrier!'

'That's the dog who goes for his dinner when the time gun fires from the Castle. You may have heard of him. He's a tough wee beast! Handles himself well in a scrap!'

'I certainly have!' replied the man who was wearing a silk top hat and an expensive tweed coat with a fur collar. 'I have it on good authority that even the Queen is aware of the little dog. Dr Lee, the minister of Greyfriars, keeps Her Majesty well informed.'

Bending down, he patted Bobby on the head. 'I'm afraid I must be going!' he said taking out his watch from inside his overcoat. 'I sincerely hope that not too many people have come to grief in this terrible disaster!'

'Do you realise who that was?' Fire Master Mitchell said, as the well dressed gentleman headed off through the crowd.

'He looked familiar. A Town Councillor?'

'No, but he does have the Freedom of the City. That was Charles Dickens the English author. He wrote *Oliver Twist*. His wife was born in the New Town.'

'Did you hear that, Bob? Maybe Mr Dickens will mention you in one of his novels! Time we were getting back to Candlemaker Row.'

When he arrived at his office the next morning, Donald opened his newspaper. 'Frightful catastrophe in the High Street! Awful loss of life!' he said, reading out the headlines to the office clerk. 'The youngster rescued by the fire brigade lay trapped under the debris for six hours. Thirty five people died in the disaster. The Lord Provost has ordered a full enquiry.'

'I'm surprised that a lot more people weren't killed. It's time these old tenements were demolished!' the clerk replied, taking off his glasses and cleaning them with his handkerchief. 'If I was the Lord Provost, I'd knock down every rat infested building in the Cowgate!'

A few days before Christmas, Maria and her father received a note from Fred Ritchie and his wife inviting them down to their house for dinner. The note explained that a cab had been booked to take them to London Street and that Donald and Bobby were also invited.

At twelve o'clock on Christmas Day, the driver knocked on the door of number twenty eight. 'That'll be our cab. Ready to go, father?' Maria asked, pulling on her gloves.

'As ready as I'll ever be!' the old man replied, putting on his bowler hat. 'How about you, Donald?'

'Lead on Macduff!' the colour sergeant said as he came into the parlour. Following the driver downstairs, Donald helped Maria and her father into the cab before instructing the little dog to jump in. Climbing on to the driving seat, the cabbie flicked his whip at the horse's rump.

Arriving at the clock maker's house, the maid ushered the guests into the drawing room. The picture frames had been decorated with ivy, laurel and holly. Brightly coloured paper chains hung on the walls. Dozens of greetings cards stood in lines along the mantelpiece on either side of the antique clock, directly above a roaring log fire. A Christmas tree topped with a fairy and decorated with glass icicles, coloured balls and candles stood in the corner.

'How are the children?' Maria enquired. 'Did they receive lots of presents?'

'Far too many, Maria! They're in the nursery right now playing with their toys!' Mrs Ritchie replied. We'll ask the nursemaid to bring them down after dinner. I'm sure they'd both love to see the little dog! Agnes is always asking about Bobby. She's never forgotten how he came to find her when the Highlanders arrived at the station.'

'Bobby's absolutely fascinated by the Christmas tree!' Maria said, going over to take a closer look at the decorations.

'He's dying to sink his teeth into one of the gingerbread men hanging from the branches!' Donald remarked. 'No matter where he goes, he's always on the scrounge for something to eat. Bob's a wee dog, but he eats like a horse! I should have named him Oliver! He keeps asking for more!'

'Cook says dinner's ready, madam,' the maid announced, holding the door open to allow the guests to make their way along the hall to the dining room.

After everyone had been served, Annie Ritchie asked the maid to bring the little dog's dinner. 'Merry Christmas, Bobby!' she said when the maid returned with a bowl filled to the brim with tasty pieces of meat. 'The dish has got your name on it! Fred had it specially made at the foundry! Now that Bobby's been served and our glasses have been filled, would you like to propose a toast, dear?' the clock maker's wife suggested turning to her husband.

'I think the toast made by Tiny Tim would be appropriate under the circumstances.' Fred replied, winking at the colour sergeant. 'Donald and Bobby will appreciate it, having recently met the country's greatest novelist!'

Raising his glass, Fred paused for a second before quoting the line created for the classic Christmas tale. 'God bless us, every one!' As Donald and the Ritchies raised their glasses in acknowledgement, Bobby barked and thumped his tail on the carpet to signal his approval.

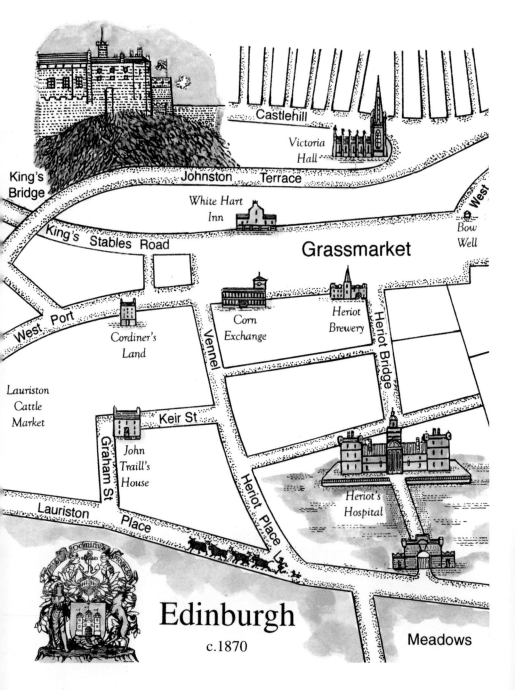

Castlehill

Victoria
Hall

King's
Bridge

Johnston Terrace

White Hart
Inn

King's Stables Road

West

Bow
Well

Grassmarket

West Port

Cordiner's
Land

Corn
Exchange

Heriot
Brewery

Heriot Bridge

Vennel

Lauriston
Cattle
Market

Keir St

Graham St

John
Traill's
House

Heriot Place

Heriot's
Hospital

Lauriston Place

Edinburgh
c.1870

Meadows

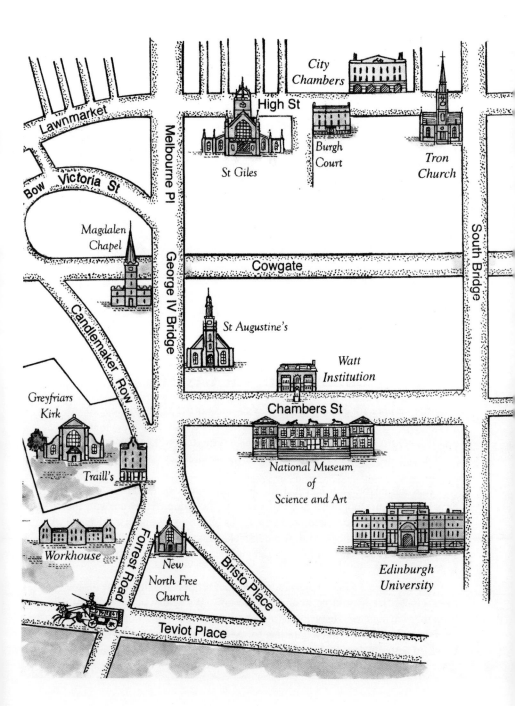

Chapter 8

BOBBY VISITS THE CASTLE

After signing for his pay at the paymaster's office, Donald stopped off at the bank on his way back from the Castle to deposit the money into his account before heading for the restaurant in Greyfriars Place. Hanging his pillbox cap on a hook on the coat rack, the soldier sat down at his usual place.

Tam the postie who had just finished his round was sitting at a table near the window supping a bowl of steaming hot soup. 'How are you the day, Donald?' John Traill enquired wiping his hands on his apron as he came through from the kitchen. 'Your usual? Steak, peas and potatoes?'

'Aye! I'll also have a slice of bread and butter and a mug of tea. How's Bob?'

'The wee beast's fine,' the restaurant keeper replied, looking at the dining room clock. 'He should be in any minute now. It's nearly one. I've got to keep the wee man fed. He brings a lot of business to this part of the town. The tourists gather at the church gate just to see him trot out when the time gun fires! I'd better make sure he can get in, or the impatient wee devil's liable to scratch the paintwork with his claws!' he added, opening the door just wide enough for the little dog to squeeze through.

'I hope the dug makes an appearance soon or we'll freeze to death!' the postman complained, wrapping his scarf tighter around his neck. 'The wind's whistlin' through that gap. If my soup gets cauld, that'll be another bowl you owe me!' Shortly after the time gun fired, the terrier padded into the dining room. Sitting down next to Donald's table, the little dog waited for the restaurant keeper to bring him his midday meal.

That evening as he sat by the fire, Donald heard a tap on the door followed by a female voice asking if he would like a cup of tea. Getting up from the carpet where he had been taking a nap, Bobby began to bark. 'Wheesht, Bob! It's only Maria!' Donald said, going to the door to let her in.

Maria was a milliner to trade. As she handed him the cup, Donald asked her if she'd been busy. 'Very!' she replied. 'Fred's very supportive. He recommends me to his customers and he's friendly with the man who owns Jenner's. Father's busy too, carrying out alteration work for the store's customers.'

'You work too hard, Maria,' Donald said as he sipped his tea. 'Would you like to visit the Castle this Saturday if you can spare the time?'

'I'd like that, Donald! I haven't been to the Castle since I was a little girl. My father took me to see Mons Meg. Could Bobby come along?' Hearing his name mentioned, the terrier lifted his shaggy little head from his paws and looked up.

'I think we could manage to get him past the sentry,' Donald replied. 'The barracks are full of dogs. Soldier's pets!'

That Saturday, Donald, Maria and Bobby set out along George IV Bridge. Turning left at the top of Melbourne Place, they made their way up the Lawnmarket towards the West Bow. Passing a group of recruiting sergeants on the lookout for volunteers, one of the bearded veterans pointed his swagger stick at the terrier and commented, 'Taking the wee dug for a walk, Colour? He should be guardin' his master's grave!'

'It's his day off!' Donald replied. 'He fancied a visit to the Castle!'

Making their way up the esplanade towards the main gate, they passed a company of infantrymen being drilled on the parade ground. 'It's a long time since I had to do that!' Donald commented. Pointing to the Half Moon Battery he told Maria that the One o'clock Gun stood beside the flagpole.

Nodding to the sentry, Donald, Maria and Bobby crossed the drawbridge into the fortress. Barking and yelping, a pack of dogs consisting of various shapes and sizes ran towards the little terrier, but decided to turn tail and head back up the brae when Bobby growled and showed his teeth.

'I vaguely recall that Mons Meg stood next to St Margaret's Chapel,' Maria said as they made their way up the cobbled brae to the Inner Gate. 'It's been so long since I visited the Castle, that it's difficult to remember.' Continuing on past the Argyle Battery, they began the climb up the steep cobbled brae through Foog's Gate to the chapel. The giant cannon, flanked on either side by a pile of huge cannonballs stood in front of the small stone building, the gun's huge barrel pointing towards the Firth of Forth.

'Mons Meg is even bigger than I remember!' Maria said, as the colour sergeant picked the little dog up and placed him on the barrel. Used to his four feet being firmly on the ground, Bobby looked round from left to right, trying to figure out the safest way to get back down. Maria laughed. 'I don't think Bobby's too happy sitting up there, Donald! I think he'd feel a lot safer on the ground!'

Strolling across to the battery wall, Maria looked over the parapet towards the shops in Princes Street and beyond to the hills of Fife. As it was Saturday afternoon, the pavements were packed with hundreds of shoppers. A row of horse-drawn cabs stood in line from the foot of the Mound to St John's Church at the West End. Wearing heavy overcoats, the drivers passed the time reading a newspaper or smoking their clay pipes, as they waited for passengers.

A small plot of land surrounded by a wall lay directly below the battery. 'That's the Dog Cemetery where the soldiers stationed in the Castle bury their pets!' Donald said, pointing to the rows of miniature headstones. 'There must be dozens of dogs buried down there by now.'

'Soldiers value loyalty, even a dog's. My father told me that one of the regiments had an elephant as a mascot which used to march through the streets with the pipe band. I wonder where they buried him?'

'If he's buried down there, the regimental pioneers must have had to dig a whacking great hole!' Donald replied. 'I'll take you to see the Crown Jewels.'

As they made their way to Crown Square, Donald spotted the master gunner standing in front of the small stone building on the edge of the Half Moon Battery, which the gunners used as a workshop. Master Gunner Taylor signalled to Donald to come across. 'This is Miss Ritchie, the clock maker's cousin!' Donald said. 'I'm showing her round the Castle. And this is Bob, the dog who goes for his dinner when the time gun fires,' the colour sergeant added, pointing to the little terrier.

'Pleased to meet you, Miss Ritchie!' the officer said, raising his right hand to salute. 'My predecessor worked with Professor Piazzi Smyth and your cousin on the time gun project. The clock he designed to fire the One o'clock Gun still keeps perfect time.'

Going through a narrow opening between the barracks block and the Palace, Donald, Maria and Bobby made their way to the Crown Room. 'I'm afraid you can't come in, Bob! No dogs allowed,' the colour sergeant said looking down at the terrier when they reached the entrance. 'We won't be long. Stay here beside the sentry box!'

Climbing the stone steps, Donald and Maria entered a wood panelled room, guarded by a warder wearing a dark blue uniform and a pillbox hat with a peak. The regalia was displayed inside a glass case surrounded by ornamental metal bars. Maria was fascinated by the Crown which lay beside the Sceptre and Sword of State on a marble slab. 'The Crown is absolutely beautiful!' she remarked.

'The gold band around the base is said to have been worn by Robert the Bruce at the Battle of Bannockburn,' the warder explained. 'The regalia was stored in that chest and the door of the Crown Room bricked up when Scotland and England were united in 1707,' he added, pointing to a massive oak trunk standing against the wall. 'The regalia was discovered when Sir Walter Scott applied for permission to have the brick wall demolished over one hundred years later.'

'Incredible!' Maria exclaimed. 'How did Sir Walter find out where the regalia was stored?'

'It's a mystery!' Donald agreed, winking at the warder. 'It couldn't have been the brickie who told him! He would have been pushing up the daisies by then. It's almost one o'clock!' he added looking at his watch. 'We'd better get back to the Half Moon Battery if you want to see the time gun firing!'

'I wouldn't want to miss that!' Maria declared. 'I'm looking forward to seeing the clock Fred designed to fire the gun!' Leaving the Crown Room and going down the stairs, Donald and Maria found Bobby sitting beside the sentry box.

'What did you think of the regalia?' the artillery officer asked Maria when they returned to the Half Moon Battery.

'Marvellous! I had no idea that the oak chest used to store the regalia would be so large.'

Master Gunner Taylor took out his pocket watch. 'Ten to one! You'll have to excuse me,' he said, making his way over to the bombardier and gunner standing by the time gun, 'It's time to start the firing procedure.'

'Get ready for the bang!' Donald warned, as the bombardier connected the lanyard to the friction-tube. 'On a clear day, the signal is so loud that it can be heard in North Berwick!'

As the minute hand reached one, the weight inside the clock cabinet dropped, activated by the signal from the observatory. Ignited by the friction-fuse, the charge which had been rammed down the barrel exploded with a tremendous roar. The heavy gun rolled backwards across the gun port apron, enveloping the Half Moon Battery in a cloud of smoke.

Maria grabbed Donald by the arm as the ground trembled beneath her feet while Bobby barked excitedly until the overpowering smell of the sulphur fumes forced him to stop and start sneezing.

'What an experience!' Maria exclaimed as the smoke began to clear. 'I felt as if I was standing in the middle of an earthquake! I'm not surprised that the signal can be heard on the opposite side of the Forth! It was so loud, they must have heard it in Aberdeen!'

'I warned you!' Donald replied, putting his arm around her shoulders. 'Are you all right? You're shaking like a jelly!'

'I'm fine, Donald! Where's Bobby?' Maria enquired, looking round the battery for the little dog. 'He's disappeared!'

'No need to worry about the wee man! Come over here and take a look!'

As Maria peered through the gun port, she spotted Bobby bounding down the esplanade as fast as his legs could carry him. 'He's heading for the restaurant!' Donald explained, pointing to the dial on the time gun's clock. 'It's one o'clock! Time for his dinner!'

Chapter 9

FOUNDER'S DAY AT HERIOT'S

It was the first Monday in June. The most important day on Heriot's school calendar. Buff Simpson felt on top of the world as he got ready to take part in the ceremony to mark the anniversary of the birth of the founder. The schoolboy was especially looking forward to this year's celebrations as he had invited Eliza Ann Traill to the annual event.

Wiping the peak of his pillbox hat with his handkerchief, Buff gave his dark blue jacket a brush before putting it on. Picking up his cornet, the youngster left the dormitory and headed down to the quadrangle where the school band had been instructed to assemble.

The north wall of the quad had been decorated with flowers and greenery for the event. The letters 'G' and 'H' in lilies had been set up on either side of Jinglin' Geordie's statue which stood in the alcove over the north archway, and a bouquet of flowers placed in the founder's hands.

Arriving in the square, Buff found the pupils, wearing new caps and uniforms lined up ready for the march to Greyfriars Church. As the janitor rang the school bell, led by the brass band and accompanied by the headmaster and members of the staff, the boys set off for the service.

Spotting Bobby sitting by the gate connecting the school grounds with the kirkyard, Buff waved his cornet at the little dog. Barking and wagging his tail, the terrier jumped up and joined the column.

Arriving at the church the headmaster, pupils and members of staff took their seats in the pews specially reserved for them. As they waited for the Lord Provost and the school governors to arrive, the boys passed conversation lozenges to the lassies from the Merchant Maiden and the Trades Maiden schools, hoping that the sweeties would increase their chances of meeting up with them later that day.

Following the service, as the boys left the church and prepared to march back to the school, they found Bobby sitting in the kirkyard. 'Coming back with us, Bobby? The kitchen staff are preparing a slap up meal!' Buff called. When he heard the word 'meal', Bobby barked and fell in beside the bass drummer.

'If Peter the gardener spots him he'll end up getting shot!' Speckie Walker remarked as they made their way up the path. 'He starts foaming at the mouth when he sees Bobby hanging around the kitchen!'

'Don't worry!' Buff assured Speckie. 'The grounds will be packed with so many people that Bobby won't be noticed.'

Buff was right. In addition to the hundreds of guests standing on the paved terrace surrounding the turreted sandstone building, the grounds had been sectioned off to accommodate the pupils from the outdoor schools connected to Heriot's. Each of the sections was packed to capacity with pupils, parents, teachers and guests.

Forming up in the quadrangle, the band got ready to march out on to the terrace. 'Right lads! Let's gie' it big licks!' the bass drummer announced. 'On the count of three!' Launching into "Cheer, Boys, Cheer!" on the third beat of the drum, the band moved smartly off across the square.

Eliza Ann who was wearing a straw hat and bright yellow dress waved to Buff as the band marched out through the archway. Reaching the edge of the terrace, the musicians came smartly to a halt and lowered their instruments, before making their way down the steps as the staff, pupils and guests clapped and cheered.

As the One o'clock Gun fired from the Half Moon Battery, led by the Lord Provost, the magistrates and school governors dressed in their ceremonial robes walked slowly up the steps, escorted by the Halberdiers carrying tasselled halberts. Raising their instruments as soon as the officials and the Lord Provost's bodyguard had taken their places, the band began playing "The Merry Month of June".

When the staff, pupils and guests had finished singing, the Lord Provost began his speech. Praising George Heriot for providing the money to build the school, he encouraged the boys to take full advantage of the educational opportunity they had been given. Raising their instruments, the band struck up again at the end of the Lord Provost's speech and the staff, pupils and guests sang "While Gratitude Fills Every Breast".

After Dr Bedford the headmaster had thanked the Lord Provost for his speech, the musicians raised their instruments and brought the ceremony to a close by playing "God Save the Queen".

As the teachers marched the pupils from the outdoor schools through the gate leading to Lauriston Place, the Lord Provost, governors, staff and boys filed into the school refectory where a special dinner had been prepared for them.

'I'd better find out where Bobby's disappeared to,' Buff said to Speckie as the pupils sat down on the wooden forms running along the side of the dining tables.

' You don't have to be the school dux to answer that one,' Speckie replied. 'He'll be in the kitchen!' Making his way to the serving hatch window in the recess at the end of the dining room, Buff asked the cook if she had seen the little dog. As she opened her mouth to reply, Bobby barked to confirm that Speckie had been right.

When the meal was over and the diners had drank a toast to the founder from the school's loving cup, Buff took his cornet back to his dormitory before going to look for Eliza Ann.

'Bobby's in the kitchen.' Buff said when he found her standing on the north terrace. 'The pupils and the old boys are going to play scudding in the quad. Would you like to watch? It can get a bit rough. It's worse than football or rugby!'

Going through the archway, Buff and Eliza Ann strolled across the square to join the spectators waiting for the game to begin. Eager to prove that they still had the skill and stamina to play the game, the former pupils taking part, lined up to buy the special balls from the boys who had spent their spare time making them during the last few weeks.

'What do the players have to do?' Eliza Ann asked Buff.

'You stoat the ball on the ground. When it bounces up, you hit it as hard as you can with your fist so that it lands on the school roof.'

'I wondered why the windows were covered with wire screens!' Eliza Ann replied with a smile. 'I thought they had been put there to keep the pupils in!'

As the game progressed, one after another, the balls got stuck in the ornamental stonework surrounding the windows and in the gutters on the roof. With only one ball left in play, the game began to get really rough, the boys and former pupils elbowing each other out of the way as they chased it round the quadrangle.

Charging across the square to get possession of the ball, the players crashed into the spectators. Eliza Ann began to get alarmed. 'I think it's time we left them to get on with the game, Buff. You're right! Scudding can be rough! I think we'll be a lot safer out on the green.'

As they made their way towards the archway, Bobby trotted into the quadrangle. Deciding to join the game, the little dog barked before dashing across the square. Picking up the ball in his mouth, the terrier turned and ran off with it. 'The cheeky wee devil!' one of the old boys shouted waving his fist. 'That ball cost me a tanner!'

Pursuing Bobby through the archway on to the terrace, the players were forced to give up as the little dog bounded down the steps into the school grounds and disappeared among the groups of children playing Kiss-in-the-Ring and Round-the-Mulberry Bush on the green.

'I wonder where Bobby's disappeared to?' Eliza Ann asked as they made their way down the terrace steps.

'He probably went back to the kirkyard to hide the ball. We can go and take a look for him if you like.'

Going through the gate connecting the school grounds with the kirkyard, as Eliza Ann and Buff made their way along the path leading to Candlemaker Row, they passed a circular stone building. A giant iron padlock was fitted to the heavy oak door.

'That's Bloody Mackenzie's Tomb! He was a terrible man! He had the Covenanters hanged in the Grassmarket.' Buff explained, pointing to the door. 'The tomb's haunted! That's why it's kept locked. Speckie's good at history. He'll tell you all about it.'

'Look, Buff!' Eliza Ann said pointing, as they approached the church gate. 'I can see Bobby!' The little dog was lying in front of the bothy, watching an artist who was sketching the gable end of the church.

'So there you are!' Buff said, looking down at Bobby.'I'm taking Eliza Ann back to the restaurant. 'Fancy coming along? I'll buy you a pie. It must be over an hour since you had your dinner! You must be feeling hungry!'

'He shouldn't be!' the artist exclaimed, glaring at the terrier. 'The greedy wee glutton's eaten all my sandwiches!'

Followed by Bobby, Buff and Eliza Ann made their way through the main gate and down the narrow cobbled lane leading to the church, before turning the corner into Greyfriars Place.

Coconut Tam was sitting at the table near the window, supping a bowl of soup. 'Hello laddie!' the street vendor said, as Buff and Eliza Ann came into the restaurant. 'Been celebrating Jinglin' Geordie's birthday?'

'Aye, Mr Simpson. That's right!' Buff replied, as Bobby trotted over to the kitchen door to find out what was cooking. 'The Lord Provost gave us a speech!'

'So the Lord Provost gave a speech! He's a great man!' John Traill said, instructing his assistant to bring Bobby a pie. 'He's the finest Lord Provost this city's ever had! He's planning to knock down the slums in the Cowgate and build new tenements. The houses will make a big difference to this part of the town.'

'And your business!' commented Tam picking up his basket and paying for his bowl of soup. 'Think o' the amount o' workmen that'll be coming in here for their dinner! You'll be able to buy the wee dug a collar oot the profits!'

Saying goodbye to Eliza Ann and thanking her for coming along, Buff made his way along Forrest Road, past the old workhouse before turning the corner into Lauriston Place. As he arrived back at the school gate the clock struck four, signalling the end of Founder's Day.

Buff thought that it was great to be alive as he removed the daisy chain which Eliza Ann had hung round his neck before going to meet his pals. He had enjoyed celebrating Jinglin' Geordie's birthday and he was looking forward to the weekend. Before leaving the restaurant, he had arranged to meet Eliza Ann at one o'clock on Sunday as they planned to visit the Castle.

Chapter 10

BOBBY IS KIDNAPPED

Although Donald no longer lived at Candlemaker Row, he still liked to treat himself to a meal at Traill's dining room when he received his wages at the end of the week. No longer a colour sergeant, he had been discharged from the Army just over a year ago, and was now working as a civilian clerk at Edinburgh Castle.

Hanging his bowler hat on a hook on the coat rack, Donald sat down at his usual place. A window cleaner sat at the corner table, reading a newspaper as he waited for a bowl of soup. 'Afternoon, Donald,' the restaurant keeper said, taking a look at the clock as he came through from the kitchen. 'What can I get you? Steak, peas and potatoes?'

'Aye!' Donald replied, taking out his watch and checking it with the clock. 'I'll also have a slice of bread and butter and a mug of tea. How's Bob keeping? I haven't seen the wee beggar for a couple of weeks!'

'Bobby's fine! He'll be in at any minute. The morning's flown in as usual. When he hears the sound of the time gun going off, he'll be here. You can bet your boots on that!'

The front door opened and John Traill's daughter came into the dining room carrying a basket of freshly laundered napkins. 'Hello, lassie. How are you? I've brought you a present,' Donald said, reaching into his jacket pocket and handing the little girl a paper bag.

'You spoil that bairn!' her father complained, wiping his hands on his apron. 'You're always bringing her sweeties and bars o' chocolate!'

'Away wi' ye, man!' the old soldier protested. 'It's only a couple of sticks o' Edinburgh rock.'

'If you keep bringing her sweeties every time you come in, it'll no' be long before she's needing false teeth!' her father replied as he went through to the kitchen to prepare Donald's dinner.

When he returned, John laid a napkin, knife and fork beside Donald's plate before sitting down on the other side of the table. 'I suppose you'll have heard that I've received a police summons!' the restaurant keeper said, pushing the salt cellar towards his plate.

If he didn't know John better, Donald would have thought that he was joking. 'The police! What's your Dad been up to, Eliza Ann?' he asked the little girl, as John's assistant arrived with his steak. 'Diggin' up bodies and selling them to the medical school? I'd be careful if I were you. Look what happened to Burke and Hare!'

'It seems that I'm Bobby's owner according to the police,' John replied, ignoring Donald's comments. 'They're expecting me to pay for the wee dog's licence.'

'That's because Bob regularly visits the restaurant. If I had bought him a collar, the summons would have been sent to me!' the old soldier said, cutting up his steak. 'The police don't realise that Bob's a stray. He's always been totally independent.'

The One o'clock Gun boomed out from the Half Moon Battery. 'Bobby should be in at any minute. He never fails to turn up on time,' John said, checking his watch and looking at the clock. 'If I pay for the licence, the neighbours who feed him might not be pleased, especially the Ritchies. As you know, Bobby's not my dog. He was coming into the dining room before I took over the lease.'

'It's a difficult situation!' Donald agreed, looking at the clock. 'It doesn't look like my wee pal's going to turn up the day! Time I was getting back to the Castle.' Going over to the coat rack, Donald took his bowler hat off the hook, paid for his meal and left the dining room.

Earlier that morning a hansom cab had stopped outside the main gate of Greyfriars Church. Jumping down from the driving seat, the cabbie made his way up the narrow lane leading to the gate and went into the bothy. 'Got the dog?' he asked James Brown who was sitting on a stool sharpening his scythe.

'Aye! Just as we arranged,' the gardener confirmed. 'I want him back here as soon as possible. The tourists expect to see the wee dog when they visit Greyfriars.'

'He'll not be gone long,' the cabbie promised. 'I'll bring him back in a couple of days!'

'You'd better!' the gardener grunted, testing the edge of his scythe with his thumb. 'He's in that basket. I've given him a sleeping draught so he'll no' gie ye' any trouble. Mind and bring the basket back. It disnae belong tae me. It belongs tae the church. Did you bring the cash?'

Handing the gardener a brown envelope, the cabbie picked up the basket. Returning to his cab he opened the door and placed the basket on the floor. Climbing up on to the driving seat, the cabbie flicked his whip at the horse's rump and shouted 'Gee up!'

Heading along George IV Bridge, the cabbie drove across the High Street and down the steep curve of the Mound towards George Street. Arriving at his destination, the cabbie jumped down from the driving seat and opened the cab door. Taking out the basket, he carried it to the front door and rang the bell. 'I've brought the dog!' he informed the housekeeper, pointing to the basket when she came downstairs to let him in.

'Mr Steell's in his studio,' the housekeeper said as he followed her upstairs. 'He's been expecting you. I'll tell him you're here!'

'You managed to get the dog!' the artist said, laying down his brush and palette, as the housekeeper ushered the cabbie into the room. 'Jolly good show!' Opening the lid of the basket, the driver lifted Bobby and laid him down on the carpet.

The little dog blinked and looked around, still groggy from the effects of the sleeping draught. The shelves were covered with bronze statuettes of dogs, horses, bulls, cows and pigs, while paintings of farmyard animals hung on the walls.

'So this is the dog everyone's talking about! The terrier I've been commissioned to paint,' Gourlay Steell said, scrutinising Bobby from every angle. 'I'm going to have quite a job making him look as sleek and well-fed as one of the pampered pets in the Royal Kennels. He doesn't look like a dog who spends much time indoors.'

Bobby bared his teeth and growled. 'He's doesn't look too happy, sir,' the cabbie observed. 'I'm sure I could find you a better model. The streets are full of strays!'

'That's exactly how I want him to look,' the painter replied. 'A picture of misery as he lies mourning on his master's grave. He'll be absolutely perfect when he's cleaned up. I'll send for you, when it's time to take him back,' he added, as the housekeeper ushered the cabbie out.

'The dog's going to need a bath,' the housekeeper said, taking a critical look at the terrier when she came back into the studio. 'He looks like a Grassmarket sweep!'

'We'll only need him for two or three days. In addition to a bath, is there anything else you can do to improve his appearance?'

'Leave him to me, sir. You'll be amazed at the difference a bar of soap, a bottle of shampoo and a set of curling tongs can make!'

Although Bobby received the best of treatment and was allowed out in the back garden, the terrier was not used to being indoors. As the little dog was being painted, he heard the sound of the One o'clock Gun firing from the Half Moon Battery. Jumping up from the satin cushion he was lying on, Bobby began barking loudly. Ringing the bell, the artist asked his housekeeper to calm the little dog down, so that he could continue with the portrait.

Three days after his arrival, the painter decided that Bobby could be returned to Greyfriars. 'Well, my wee pal!' the artist said, laying down his brush and palette. 'I've enjoyed your company but you've been here long enough. I don't think we need detain you any longer. Time you were re-united with your friends!'

Although the little dog had got used to eating the best of butcher meat and being shampooed, perfumed and pampered, Bobby didn't need any encouragement to jump into the cab, when the driver arrived to pick him up.

As soon as the cab halted near the top of Candlemaker Row and the cabbie opened the door, Bobby leapt out and headed for the restaurant in Greyfriars Place at top speed.

The Traills were overjoyed to see the little dog. John immediately sent his assistant to inform the Ritchies that the terrier had returned. 'Bobby looks different since he disappeared!' Eliza Ann exclaimed. 'Look at his shiny, curly coat, Daddy. He looks grand enough to win first prize at a dog show!'

'Any idea where Bob's been for the last few days?' Donald enquired when he came into the restaurant at the end of the week.

'No idea! It's a bit of a mystery,' the restaurant keeper replied as he brought Donald's steak and potatoes through from the kitchen. 'But you can tell by his appearance that he's been well looked after.'

'I wouldn't be surprised if the gardener had something to do with it!' Donald replied. 'Not only does he sell photographs of Bob to the tourists, he spins them the tale that he's guarding his master's grave. The visitors even hand the auld rascal money to buy the wee man his dinner. It won't be long before Bob appears on posters advertising Spratt's dog biscuits!'

Chapter 11

BOBBY GETS A LICENCE

On his way to work at the Castle, Donald bought a copy of *The Scotsman* from the newsboy at the top of Victoria Street. Scanning the pages as soon as he reached his office, he found what he was looking for - the report on the hearing at the Burgh Court to establish the identity of Bobby's owner.

'Looks like the reporter's been speaking to the gardener at the kirk,' Donald said, passing the paper to his assistant. 'According to the article, Bob first appeared at the funeral of a man called Gray and he's been sleeping on his grave for the last eight and a half years.'

'The dog's in danger of being put down, if no one comes forward to pay for the licence,' the clerk replied, as he read the article. 'The police disapprove of stray animals running around the city!'

The following day at quarter to one, as John Traill was sweeping the pavement outside his restaurant, a tall, thin man wearing a dark grey overcoat and a bowler hat approached him. 'Good afternoon, Mr Traill. My name's Alexander Macpherson. I'm the City Officer. The Lord Provost was extremely interested in the article on the terrier which appeared in yesterday's *Scotsman*. According to the article the dog frequents your restaurant. As Mr Chambers is also a director of the Scottish Society for the Prevention of Cruelty to Animals, he's instructed me to bring the dog down to his house.'

'I can't guarantee that Bobby will go with you, Mr Macpherson,' John replied, looking at his watch. 'If you can spare a few minutes, you'll soon find out. Can I get you a cup of tea or coffee while you're waiting?'

Two minutes after the time gun fired, the little dog trotted into the dining room. 'You've got a visitor, Bobby!' the restaurant keeper said as he laid the little dog's dinner dish down in front of him. 'This is Mr Macpherson. He'd like you to go with him to meet the Lord Provost.'

Although the city officer tried to coax Bobby out on to the pavement, the terrier would not be persuaded. 'He might change his mind if my wife and daughter were to go with you,' John suggested. 'She's in the kitchen. I'll ask her.'

Returning to the dining room, John told the official that they would be happy to accompany Bobby to the Lord Provost's house. While Mrs Traill and Eliza Ann changed into their Sunday clothes, the city officer went outside to hail a cab.

Arriving at the Lord Provost's house at the city's west end, the maidservant took the visitors into the drawing room. 'A pleasure to meet you and your daughter, Mrs Traill,' Mrs Chambers said, getting up from the sofa. 'Please sit down. My husband and I are grateful to you for coming along. Would you like a cup of tea?' she enquired, ringing the bell for the maidservant. 'Perhaps Eliza Ann would prefer a glass of milk or orange juice?'

'So this is the dog who has been appearing in the press!' the Lord Provost said, putting on his spectacles to get a better look as the terrier settled down on the drawing room carpet. 'What do you suggest we should do Harriet?' he asked his wife.

'We can't allow Bobby to be put down, William! It would be detrimental to the image of the city. According to the newspaper article, he's been sleeping on his master's grave for eight and a half years. Bobby is already well known locally. The newspaper article is bound to turn him into a celebrity. If he was put down, can you imagine the public outcry which would result!'

'We appreciate you bringing Bobby along, Mrs Traill. I agree with my wife. I think we should purchase the licence for the dog. He's not only an asset to the people of Greyfriars, but to the City of Edinburgh!'

'You won't have to persuade the Council to give him the Freedom of the City, William,' Mrs Chambers added with a smile. 'I've been told that he already goes exactly where he pleases! Would you like to see our dog, Eliza Ann?'

Ringing the bell, the Lord Provost's wife instructed the maidservant to bring the spaniel to the drawing room. 'This is Fanny!' she announced as the little dog trotted in. 'She's absolutely spoiled. She doesn't have to go foraging for food like Bobby!' When he heard the word 'food' Bobby lifted his head from his paws and barked. 'I think he'd like a biscuit, William,' Mrs Chambers said.

'I'm sure you're right, dear,' her husband replied. 'You'd better ask Chrissie to fetch the tin. He looks like a hungry wee beast. I'm sure he'd also like a saucer of milk.'

The Lord Provost was as good as his word. The following week, the postman delivered a parcel to the restaurant at Greyfriars Place. Opening the box, John Traill took out a brand new leather collar with the inscription 'Greyfriars Bobby, from the Lord Provost, 1867, licenced' engraved on a brass plate.

'Even the gardener at Heriot's can't chase him now, Daddy!' Eliza Ann declared when her father showed her the collar. 'He can go into the school grounds whenever he likes. Why do you think the Lord Provost bought Bobby a licence?' the little girl asked, as she buckled the collar round the little dog's neck.

'The Lord Provost had to fend for himself when he was young,' her father replied. 'He and his brother had to rely on their wits to survive. Perhaps that's why he decided to protect the wee dog.'

As Mrs Chambers predicted, the newspaper article turned Bobby into a national celebrity. Visitors travelled from every part of the country to see the little dog who had now been nicknamed Greyfriars Bobby.

Several months later, one of John Traill's customers who worked as a cleaner at the National Gallery came into the restaurant when he had finished his shift. 'Morning, Sandy!' John said wiping his hands on his apron, as he had just been poking the fire. 'A cold morning but what else can we expect at this time of the year. Your usual? A bowl of Scotch broth?'

'Aye! I'll also have a slice o' bread and a mug o' tea!' Sandy replied, sitting down at the table next to the fire. 'How's the wee dug? I've heard he's been suffering from a sore back.'

'He's not getting any younger, but he's fit enough!' John said, wiping the table with a cloth. 'The wee beast's a tourist attraction! The visitors gather at the church gate to see him trot out for his dinner when the time gun fires. He's getting to be nearly as famous as Mons Meg!'

'There's a painting of Bobby on show in the North Room,' Sandy said as he peeled off his woollen mittens. 'It's part of the Royal Scottish Academy's annual exhibition.'

'I'll tell the wife!' John replied, laying Sandy's bowl of soup down on the table. 'Eliza Ann would definitely like to see it. I'd like to see the painting myself.'

The following Saturday, dressed in their Sunday best, the Traills headed along George IV Bridge. Crossing over to Bank Street they headed down the Mound to the National Gallery which had been designed to resemble a Greek temple. Escorting his wife and daughter up the front steps into the entrance hall, John asked the attendant for directions to the North Room.

'Look Daddy! It's Bobby!' Eliza Ann cried, clapping her hands together with excitement when she spotted the painting which was attracting a lot of attention. 'Doesn't he look grand! You would think that he belonged to the Lord Provost!' Mounted in a gilt frame, the painting showed the little terrier lying on a grave with his head on his paws, looking extremely fed up.

'Looks like the mystery of Bobby's disappearance when he vanished last year has been solved,' John said examining the portrait closely.

'You're right, Daddy. Look at Bobby's shiny, curly coat! That's exactly how he looked when he came back to the restaurant after he went missing!'

A group of art lovers were also admiring the painting. 'It's extremely well executed,' observed a long-haired young man wearing a black velvet jacket. 'Not as competent as Landseer, but a professional piece of brushwork just the same.'

'Totally agree with you, Louis old chap!' his companion replied, scrutinising the painting through his monocle. 'The dog's a pedigree! No doubt about it! I'd hazard a guess that he's related to one of Her Majesty's Skye terriers!'

Overhearing the comment, John Traill couldn't resist taking the opportunity to join in. 'I'm well acquainted with that dog!' John announced, pointing at the painting. 'He comes into my restaurant every day for his dinner. He's related to Black Bob of Kyleakin.'

'The prize-winning Skye terrier?' exclaimed the art lover, removing his monocle in astonishment.

'Afraid not!' the restaurant keeper replied, winking at his daughter. 'Black Bob MacTavish, the Grassmarket sweep!'

Chapter 12

A VERY IMPORTANT PERSON VISITS GREYFRIARS

As John Traill was working in the kitchen, he heard the bell above the front door tinkling. 'Sounds like we've got a customer, Agnes,' he said to his assistant. 'Keep an eye on the soup!' Putting down the spoon he had been using to stir the pot, he went through to the dining room where he found a cabbie wearing a heavy overcoat, bowler hat and muffler, warming his hands at the fire.

'Can I help you?' John enquired, offering him a menu. 'A bowl of soup? A pot of Scotch broth is presently simmering on the stove!'

'Another time perhaps, Mr Traill! I'm here on business. Have you any idea where I can find the dog who comes in here when the time gun fires?'

'He'll be in shortly. Bobby arrives for his dinner precisely after one!' John said pointing to the clock.

'Two ladies and a gentleman are waiting in the kirkyard to see him! The ladies are staying at the Balmoral in Princes Street across from the Castle,' the cabbie explained. 'They've travelled up by train from London.'

'They've come a long way! In that case I'd better show you where the wee beast can be found!' Putting on his hat and overcoat as it was a cold

November day, John left Agnes to look after the restaurant, and accompanied the cab driver to the kirkyard.

'Good afternoon,' John said, introducing himself to a distinguished looking gentleman wearing a top hat and overcoat, standing with two ladies outside the bothy next to the main gate. 'I'm John Traill. Your driver informs me that you're looking for Greyfriars Bobby.'

'That's correct, Mr Traill,' the gentleman replied. 'My name is Hay. I'm secretary of the Scottish Society for the Prevention of Cruelty to Animals. This is Lady Burdett-Coutts and Mrs Brown,' he added introducing his female companions. 'They've travelled all the way from London to meet the famous terrier, so often mentioned in the papers.'

John glanced at the tall elegant lady. He knew exactly who she was, as he had read about her in the newspapers. Not only was Lady Burdett-Coutts the wealthiest woman in Britain, she was a close friend of the Queen. Her grandfather had been Provost of Edinburgh and she had provided Dr Livingstone, the African explorer, with the money to build a paddle steamer.

'Can you take us to the spot where we might find the little dog, Mr Traill?' Lady Burdett-Coutts enquired.

'The wee beast can generally be found at the back of the kirkyard. He's a tourist attraction! The visitors are already assembling to see him trot out,' John replied, pointing to a group of men, women and children standing outside the church's front gate. 'If you'd be kind enough to follow me, we'll see if we can find him.'

As John predicted, they found Bobby close to the gate leading to Heriot's, searching for a bone he had buried the previous day. 'So this is the terrier who faithfully guards his master's grave,' Lady Burdett-Coutts said, looking down at the little dog who was hard at work trying to dig a hole in the frozen ground. 'His story has been featured in newspapers and magazines all over the world.'

The One o'clock Gun suddenly boomed out from the Half Moon Battery. As soon as he heard the signal, the terrier immediately stopped digging and headed off like a bullet down the gravel path leading to the church gate.

'You'll have to excuse Bobby's bad manners,' John explained, 'The One o'clock Gun is his dinner signal. When the time gun fires, he heads for my restaurant. Bobby's one of my best customers. He even has his own bowl with his name on it!'

'Do you have any details on the history of the dog, Mr Traill?' Lady Burdett-Coutts enquired, as they walked back along the pathway to the church gate. 'Have you any idea who originally owned the terrier?'

'He was already well known in the district before I took over the restaurant,' John explained. 'The church gardener believed that he belonged to a man called Gray who lodged in the Old Town. Personally I believe that Bobby could have belonged to anyone. The butcher, baker or candlestick maker!'

As they passed the bothy, the restaurant keeper pointed to the front door of the building on the left hand side of the narrow lane leading to the church gate. 'Colour Sergeant Scott who lodged at number twenty eight fed the dog. Bobby was also friendly with a tailor called Robert Ritchie who lived there. The dog sometimes slept in the tailor's flat at night. Both the gardener and the tailor have passed away, so I'm afraid you'll have difficulty in finding out much more. The gardener is buried in Greyfriars. His wife couldn't afford a headstone. The tailor's buried in the Grange Cemetery on the other side of town.'

'The ladies are staying at the Balmoral Hotel, Mr Traill. If you find out anything which might help us with our enquiries you can contact me here,' Mr Hay informed the restaurant keeper handing him his card, before following his female companions through the gate to the waiting cab.

When she returned to her hotel, Lady Burdett-Coutts immediately wrote a letter to the Council asking for permission to set up a memorial to Bobby's owner in Greyfriars Kirkyard. Ringing the bell for the hotel's page boy, she instructed him to take it to the post office.

'According to Lady Burdett-Coutts, the dog's owner was an old soldier called Robert Gray,' the chairman of the Plans and Works Committee said, handing the letter to one of his clerks after he had read it.

'I wonder where she got the information? It's a bit of a mystery. According to the newspaper article, the owner lived in the Old Town,' the clerk replied scratching his head. 'It seems an odd coincidence that his name was Gray, as if the name had been thought up by the reporter on the spur of the moment. Gray sounds similar to Greyfriars.'

'Unfortunately she doesn't say,' the chairman said, reading the letter again. 'You'd better check the burial records. As you know, her ladyship is a close friend of the Queen. If you manage to find out who the dog belonged to, you might end up with a knighthood!'

Consulting the burial ledgers, the clerk found that although a carter named Robert Gray had died about the time that Bobby was said to have appeared in the graveyard, he had been buried in Preston Street Cemetery on the south side of the city.

Later that morning, just before his lunch break, the clerk returned to the chairman's office. 'According to the records, a police constable named John

Gray was buried in Greyfriars in February 1858, but the newspaper article seems to indicate that the dog's owner was buried several months later,' he reported. 'I'm afraid the church gardener is no longer with us so I can't ask him!'

'I see!' the city official replied stroking his moustache. 'In that case send her ladyship a letter stating that although we have no record of the owner being buried in Greyfriars, we have no objection to a memorial stone being erected.'

'I'll have it drafted right away, sir!' As he left the office, he turned and added 'I could check with the police to enquire if the terrier was officially employed as a watch dog.'

'Not a good idea, Simkin!' the chairman replied as he toyed with his watch chain. 'It was the police who delivered the summons to John Traill! The superintendent of police would not be pleased, if it was to be revealed that the terrier was a member of the force! I'm afraid, we can spend no more time trying to locate the dog's owner! The department has a lot more important matters to attend to!'

'So you wish me to proceed no further, sir!' the clerk said as he made his way to the door.

'That's correct!' the city official replied, checking his watch as the One o'clock Gun fired from the Castle. 'Now that the dog's a celebrity, historians will be arguing about the identity of his owner in a hundred years time. Mark my words! To avoid wasting valuable time and to preserve the reputation of the city constabulary, it would be a good idea to let sleeping dogs lie!'

Chapter 13

BOBBY AND THE CITY TRAMS

As Eliza Ann was taking Bobby for a walk, she spotted a group of men and women standing outside the City Chambers holding posters and placards. 'I wonder what's going on, Bobby?' she said to the little dog. Waiting until a horse-drawn omnibus had rattled past, Eliza Ann and Bobby crossed the busy street to find out.

'Is that Greyfriars Bobby, little girl?' a lady dressed in a grey topcoat and black bonnet enquired, pointing to the terrier, when she spotted Eliza Ann reading one of the protestor's placards. 'That dog has friends in high places. Perhaps they could help us prevent the Council from ruining the city by allowing tram lines to be laid along the streets!' Handing Eliza Ann a leaflet, she asked her if she would be kind enough to show it to her father.

Returning to the restaurant, Eliza Ann found Donald sitting at his usual place, enjoying a meal of steak and potatoes. 'Hello lassie!' Donald said, laying down his knife and fork as he patted the little dog on the head. 'Been out for a walk? How's Bob?' Pleased to see his old friend, the terrier barked and wagged his tail.

'He's keeping just fine, Mr Scott,' the little girl replied, removing her bonnet. 'He's getting to be really famous! Daddy received a letter last week from a little girl called Eleanor who lives in America, asking for Bobby's photograph! That right, Bobby?' The terrier barked to confirm Eliza Ann's statement. 'A lady outside the City Chambers asked me to give you this, Daddy,' she added, handing her father the leaflet.

Sitting down at Donald's table the restaurant keeper polished his spectacles on his apron, before putting them on. 'The Council's proposing to build a tram line, linking the town with Leith and Portobello!' John said, handing the old soldier the leaflet, after reading it carefully.

'Seems a waste of money. The city's already got an adequate transport system,' Donald replied as he scrutinised the details. 'There's even a steam bus running between Edinburgh and Leith.'

'The trams won't be steam driven. According to the leaflet, the cars will be pulled by horses!'

'I don't think that's a good idea,' Donald replied, handing the leaflet back to John. 'The city's built on too many hills! The gradients will put a tremendous strain on the animals.'

'There's no doubt about that,' the restaurant keeper agreed. 'Even a steam bus has trouble getting up to the top of Leith Street!' Picking up Donald's plate, he took it through to the kitchen.

Despite the public's protests, the Edinburgh Street Tramways Company received permission to proceed with the project. Wasting no time, the company's workmen began laying a line from Bernard Street at the foot of Leith Walk to Haymarket at the city's west end.

Although his uncle had passed away, Fred Ritchie continued to keep in touch with his cousin. Following his visits, the clock maker regularly popped into the restaurant at Greyfriars Place. 'How's Bobby?' Fred asked when he called in for a cup of coffee.

'Like the rest of us, he's not getting any younger! He's got most of his teeth but he's still having trouble with his back. Mary took him down to the Dick Vet last week. The professor's had a good look at him, but there's not a lot he can do. He'll be out in the kirkyard. We can go round and see him if you've got a minute to spare.'

'I'd better!' Fred replied. 'Agnes and Jamie will expect a report when I get back home!' Removing his apron, John went through to the kitchen and put on his jacket and bowler hat.

'How's the new tram system working?' John enquired as they walked along the path to the spot where Bobby liked to hunt for rats. 'I've heard that the company now plans to lay a line along Chambers Street.'

'The trams are giving the omnibuses a fair old run for their money, there's no doubt about that, but the company seems to regard the horses as expendable. As you know, the route from the bottom of Leith Walk to the General Post Office is uphill all the way. The gradient outside our shop is particularly steep and narrow. Although trace horses are hitched to the cars to assist the teams, the strain on the animals is considerable!'

'Is it true that the tram wheels have not been fitted with protective guards?' John enquired. 'According to an article I read in the paper, a pedestrian nearly lost a leg outside the Royal Institution where the line runs close to the pavement at the foot of the Mound. I've also been told that the cars are being overloaded, especially during the rush hours!'

'I'm afraid that's correct. The members of the SSPCA are doing all they can to remedy the unfortunate situation. Lady Burdett-Coutts is lending her support to the campaign.' Finding Bobby at the far side of the kirkyard, John called out to the little dog. Pleased to see the clock maker, Bobby stopped searching for rats and trotted across to greet his old friend.

The following day, just before one, the lady who had given Eliza Ann the leaflet, came into the restaurant. 'Good afternoon Mr Traill. This is Mr Hay, the secretary of the SSPCA,' she explained, introducing the gentleman accompanying her. 'Our members plan to march along Princes Street on Saturday to protest against the shocking treatment the tramway horses are receiving!'

'I met Mr Hay some time ago!' John replied, shaking the secretary's hand. 'He brought Lady Burdett-Coutts to Greyfriars to see Bobby. Nice to see you again.'

'It's a pleasure to meet you too, Mr Traill! Although the horses' collars are fitted with bells and the drivers issued with a whistle to keep the tram lines clear of traffic, the strain on the horses increases when carts and cyclists cut in front of the teams, forcing them to stop,' Mr Hay added. 'We were wondering if Bobby would lead the march as he's so well known. The little dog's support would be greatly appreciated!'

'I'll certainly ask my wife if Bobby can take part,' the restaurant keeper promised, as the time gun fired and the terrier trotted in for his midday meal. 'I'm totally opposed to the way the horse teams are being treated! It's an absolute disgrace! How can I get in touch with you?'

'You can contact me at our office in North Bank Street, Mr Traill!' the secretary replied, handing over his card. 'Many thanks for your help! I can assure you that it is very much appreciated!'

That evening, as they were getting ready for bed, John told his wife that he had received a visit from Mr Hay, and that he had enquired if he could have permission for Bobby to lead the march. Not only did Mary Traill give her consent, she decided that she would like to take part.

Arriving at the foot of the Mound on Saturday morning, Eliza Ann, her mother and Bobby found the square next to the Royal Institution packed with protestors. In addition to representatives from the city's organisations and schools, members of the SSPCA had travelled from all over Scotland to support the campaign.

'Looks like the whole city's turned out!' Mrs Traill remarked. Spotting Heriot's school band waiting for the order to march off, Eliza Ann waved to Buff and his pals, as the chairman of the SSPCA escorted Bobby to the head of the procession.

As the demonstrators waited for the One o'clock Gun to fire, signalling the march to begin, the chairman read out a letter from Lady Burdett-Coutts wishing them success with their campaign.

'Keep a tight grip on Bobby's leash when we march along Princes Street!' Mrs Traill advised her daughter. 'Bobby's not only a celebrity, he's now a national treasure! We don't want him getting run over by a tram!'

The sound of the One o'clock Gun thundered out from the Half Moon Battery. Used to going for his dinner when the time gun fired, Bobby lurched forward, pulling Eliza Ann with him. Spotting the little dog moving off, the bass drummer thumped his drum and the band struck up.

Followed by hundreds of demonstrators carrying placards and banners, Bobby, Eliza Ann, her mother, the chairman and committee members of the SSPCA, led by Heriot's school band set off along Princes Street towards the West End.

When Eliza Ann and her mother returned to the restaurant later that afternoon, John Traill asked his daughter if the demonstration had been a success.'It certainly was, Daddy! We marched along Princes Street to the Sinclair fountain outside St John's Church.'

'After all that marching you'll be needing a snack!' her father said, as she took off her bonnet. 'Bobby too! He gave up his dinner break to take part in the protest!'

'The chairman of the SSPCA took Mummy and me to a big hotel at the West End and bought us a three-course dinner!' Eliza Ann replied.'The waiter brought Bobby a big bowl of scraps!' Bobby's ears pricked up when he heard the word 'scraps'.

'Looks like he's still feeling hungry,' the restaurant keeper said, as the little grey terrier wagged his tail and licked his lips. 'Agnes!' he shouted through to the kitchen. 'Bring the wee dog a meat pie!'

Chapter 14

BOBBY'S DRINKING FOUNTAIN

Bobby's health was beginning to fail. The terrier no longer trotted round the district visiting the shops and his old friends. One evening, two weeks after Hogmanay, as the little dog was lying in front of the fire, Mary Traill came into the living room. 'Bobby's very quiet, John,' she said to her husband who was reading the evening paper. 'I can hardly hear him breathing.' Bending down to take a look at the little grey dog, she turned to John, her eyes filled with tears. 'Bobby's gone! The children will be very upset if they see him.'

Laying down the newspaper, the restaurant keeper rose from his armchair. 'You're right, Mary,' he confirmed. 'The wee dog's no longer with us. He's taken his last nap!' Although the clock on the mantelpiece was ticking, it seemed as though time was standing still.

'I could put him in the broom cupboard until we decide where he's to be buried,' John suggested, unbuckling Bobby's collar. Going into the hall, he put on his hat and coat. 'I won't be long, Mary!' he called to his wife as he opened the front door. 'I'm just going along to Donald Scott's! He's entitled to be the first to know!'

Making his way to the flat in Bristo Place where the old soldier lived, John knocked on the door. 'Where do you think we should bury him?' the restaurant keeper asked, showing Donald the collar, after delivering the bad news. 'Mary would like Bobby to be laid to rest in the kirkyard, but I can't see the authorities allowing a dog to be buried near the church.'

'The small plot of land behind the main gate would be ideal. I doubt if anyone would object to him being laid to rest there. Bury him under the tree! That's where I first spotted the poor wee beast when he came into the kirkyard shivering wi' the cold. The school joiner would knock up a coffin!'

The following afternoon just as it was getting dark, a group of John's friends gathered in his flat behind the restaurant. 'The gardener and the grave diggers will have gone by now,' John said looking at his watch. 'It should be safe enough to bury Bobby.'

Opening the window, one by one, the members of the burial party climbed out into the kirkyard. Carrying the little dog's body to the flower plot in front of the church, the restaurant keeper dug a hole near the tree which stood not far from the centre.

After the grave had been filled in, John placed a small headstone chiselled with the words 'Greyfriars Bobby' over the spot. Thanking his friends for their help, the restaurant keeper told them that he'd hand the little dog's collar into the office at the front gate in the morning.

Although Lady Burdett-Coutts had decided to abandon her plan to set up a memorial in Greyfriars kirkyard, she applied to the Council asking permission to erect a drinking fountain at the junction of Candlemaker Row and George IV Bridge.

Receiving a letter permitting her to proceed, a squad of workmen arrived to lay the foundation. When the pedestal had been set up, a bronze statue of Bobby was placed on top.

'What do you think of the wee dog's statue?' Donald asked Eliza Ann when he came into the restaurant at the end of the week. 'Think it looks like Bob?'

'Aye, Mr Scott! It certainly does!' the little girl replied. 'I like it very much! The statue looks exactly like Bobby when he returned to the restaurant after he disappeared. He looks good enough to win first prize at a dog show! I had a drink from one of the metal cups.'

The One o'clock Gun fired from the Half Moon Battery. 'Time I was getting back to work,' Donald said, pushing back his chair and rising from the table. 'I hope you cleaned the cup with your hankie first, hen!' he commented as he put on his bowler hat. 'Coconut Tam might have been using it!'

Several months later as the restaurant keeper was working in the kitchen, he heard the bell over the front door tinkling. Laying down the brush he used for cleaning the pots, he went through to the dining room. A telegram boy was standing in front of the fire warming his hands.

'You've got a telegram!' announced Coconut Tam who was sitting at the table in the corner. 'Mind and gie' the laddie a tip!' Opening the telegram, the restaurant keeper found it was from Angela Burdett-Coutts who had now been made a Baroness, inviting the Traills to the unveiling of the drinking fountain.

Just before noon in the middle of November, a small group of Bobby's friends including Donald, Maria and the Traills gathered round the little dog's memorial. The bronze plaque on the front of the pedestal read: 'A tribute to the affectionate fidelity of Greyfriars Bobby. In 1858 this faithful dog followed the remains of his master to Greyfriars Churchyard and lingered near the spot until his death in 1872. With permission erected by Baroness Burdett-Coutts.'

Before leaving for London, the Baroness and her companion Hannah Brown paid John Traill a visit. 'We'd like you to accept this copy of *Little Fan*,' she said, handing the restaurant keeper a small book. 'It's signed by Hannah and myself. As you know the campaign to prevent the tram horses from being abused has been successful. We can't thank you and your family enough for the help you have given us.'

Early the following year, the Traill family received an invitation from the City Chambers to attend a special ceremony. The Town Council had decided to award Baroness Burdett-Coutts the Freedom of the City and the Traills had been invited to the Assembly Rooms to see her receive the city's highest honour.

Wearing their Sunday best, the Traills climbed into the cab which had been booked by the restaurant owner to take them to the ceremony. Flicking his whip at the horse's rump, the driver headed off along George IV Bridge through the busy traffic, down the Mound and across to Hanover Street before turning left into George Street.

The auditorium and gallery were packed with guests, including William Brodie who had sculpted the statue of Bobby sitting on the drinking fountain. An organ was playing as the Traills were escorted to their seats by one of the city's High Constables.

Potted plants stood at intervals along the front of the stage which was draped with red cloth. A portrait of the Baroness's grandfather Provost Coutts, surrounded by a cluster of flags stood in the centre, while two large Union

Jacks had been set up at an angle of seventy five degrees at each end of the platform.

'Look, Mummy!' Eliza Ann cried, pointing to the group of special guests. 'It's the Lord Provost who bought Bobby his licence and collar! His wife's here too!'

'Don't point, Eliza Ann! Mr Chambers is no longer Lord Provost,' her mother explained. 'Being Lord Provost's not like running a restaurant. You don't get to keep the job for very long!'

At one o'clock, as the time gun fired from the Half Moon Battery, the Baillies and Councillors dressed in their scarlet and ermine robes filed slowly on to the platform and took their seats behind the special guests.

Shortly after one, a civic official escorted by ceremonial sword bearers filed on to the stage, carrying the city's gold mace. The guests rose to their feet, as the tall, elegant lady who had devoted her life to improving the conditions of the poor and protecting animals walked out on to the stage accompanied by the Lord Provost and gave her a standing ovation.

Praising the Baroness for her generosity and dedication, Lord Provost Cowan presented her with a silver casket embossed with the arms of the city. When she had finished thanking the Lord Provost for the honour which had been bestowed on her, the guests including the Traills rose to their feet and gave three hearty cheers.

Arriving back at the restaurant, while her father paid the cabbie, Eliza Ann crossed over to the red granite drinking fountain at the top of Candlemaker Row. 'Baroness Burdett-Coutts has been given the Freedom of the City, Bobby!' she said looking up at the statue of the little dog. 'We've just come back from the ceremony in the Music Hall.'

Going back across the road, Eliza Ann found her father waiting for her. 'Don't tell your mother,' John Traill said as he opened the dining room door to let her in. 'I think I must be seeing things!'

'What do you mean, Daddy?' Eliza Ann asked as they entered the restaurant.

'It could have been my imagination or a trick of the light,' her father replied. 'But when you were standing at the fountain talking to the wee dog, I could swear I saw him wag his tail!'